"I write tales of adventure in paradise..."

He stood so close, Susan could feel the warmth of him, could see the haunted longing in his eyes. With infinite slowness, his face lowered. When his mouth finally closed over hers, she was totally unprepared for the devastating jolt to her senses. Her lips parted, accepting the deep probings of his tongue as a moan escaped from her throat.

When he released her, his breath was warm on her cheek.

"The pleasure of a beautiful woman's kiss," he said softly, kissing the tip of her nose, "is one of life's pure delights. But nothing lasts forever, my little romantic friend. Nothing."

Dear Reader,

Your enthusiastic reception of SECOND CHANCE AT LOVE has inspired all of us who work on this special romance line and we thank you.

Now there are *six* brand new, exciting SECOND CHANCE AT LOVE romances for you each month. We've doubled the number of love stories in our line because so many readers like you asked us to. So, you see, your opinions, your ideas, what you think, really count! Feel free to drop me a note to let me know your reactions to our stories.

Again, thanks for so warmly welcoming SECOND CHANCE AT LOVE and, please, *do* let me hear from *you*!

With every good wish,

Carolyn Nichols

Carolyn Nichols
SECOND CHANCE AT LOVE
The Berkley/Jove Publishing Group
200 Madison Avenue
New York, New York 10016

P.S. Because your opinions *are* so important to us, I urge you to fill out and return the questionnaire in the back of this book.

Second Chance at Love™

SAPPHIRE ISLAND
DIANE CRAWFORD

A
SECOND CHANCE AT LOVE
BOOK

First edition published January 1982

First printing

"Second Chance at Love" and the butterfly emblem are trademarks belonging to Jove Publications, Inc.

Printed in the United States of America

Second Chance at Love books are published by
The Berkley/Jove Publishing Group,
200 Madison Avenue, New York, NY 10016

To my husband Bill
my love, my life

CHAPTER
One

THE SMALL SEAPLANE BANKED, swooping beneath puffy cotton clouds, and Susan McRay's breath caught in her throat. Below, surfacing like a jewel in the blue Pacific, the island shimmered in the morning sunlight. Shades of emerald velvet gave way to a broken shoreline of white sandy beaches, secluded coves, and treacherous cliffs where turquoise water exploded into frothy lace.

Susan braced herself for the landing, feeling euphoric at the thought of spending the next three weeks in this tropical paradise, of being able to relax and unwind, soak up the sun, dabble at her painting, and, hopefully, forget Paul Shelley ever existed. In addition to being the best landlady in the world, Essie

Knight, sitting next to her, was a dear friend, and Susan would be forever grateful for her invitation.

"I wouldn't have invited you if I couldn't afford to take you along as my guest," Essie had reasoned several weeks before. "I'm more than comfortably well off, and how I spend my money is my business. If it would make you feel better, you can consider it a three-week mini-job with all expenses paid. Think of it as a mission of mercy. I've got to talk that stubborn sister-in-law of mine into giving up her island retreat and moving Stateside. Her husband died years ago and, except for her son Kaleb, who hops back and forth between the island and the states, she lives alone with just a few servants. But she refuses to let go of the island. I'm going to need all the help I can get to convince her to move to San Francisco." Essie had hitched a brow and pursed her lips. "Besides a change of scenery, you need a place to lose yourself, my dear. Of course it won't be forever, but it seems to me three weeks ought to be long enough to heal a few wounds, eh?"

Susan didn't think her wounds would ever heal, but the trip might make them bearable. Maybe here she could forget the night she'd found her fiancé entertaining a beautiful, half-dressed blonde in his apartment.

She had loved Paul completely and given all there was to give. But he had lied to her and deceived her and in one devastating blow, he had destroyed her world.

Susan's thoughts were interrupted when the seaplane landed as softly as a gull on the crystal water, and taxied toward one of the secluded coves she had observed from the air. A rickety pier stretched out from shore, and standing on it, looking as bright as the morning sun and as colorful as a tropical bouquet, Helen, Essie's sister-in-law, waited, waving her arms in welcome. A tall Samoan stood next to her.

Susan and Essie stepped off the plane to a whirlwind of greetings, and Susan found herself smothered in Helen Knight's exuberant arms. The woman was tall—close to six feet—and Susan had to crook her neck to look up at her vivid sea-green eyes and hair the color of a copper penny, just touched with gray. Helen's smile was infectious.

"Well, Essie Mae, you weren't kidding when you said your little friend was beautiful," she beamed, gently touching Susan's cheek. "Oh, but you didn't tell me her eyes were the color of Cattleya orchids! How lovely with her warm chestnut hair."

"Her eyes are the color of purple pansies," Essie contradicted with a scowl. "Pansies grow in the United States . . . where you should be living, dear Helen."

"Now Essie, you know I don't want to get into that," Helen announced irritably. "Besides, this is American Samoa, an unincorporated territory of the United States, and that's close enough for me."

"But not close enough for me," Essie pressed, still scowling up at her sister-in-law. "Hmmmmm, you've put on weight, dear Helen."

"Talofa," the Samoan man next to them said, taking Susan's hand and bowing. "Forgive them. They argue when they are together and weep tears when apart."

"Talofa means 'welcome' in Samoan," Helen interjected. "This is Sam Kahanakee, my right-hand man and friend. Sam, this pretty little lady is Susan McRay, a friend of Miss Essie's."

"Susan rents one of the upstairs apartments in my nice, big apartment building in San Francisco," it was Essie's turn to interject. "Nice big apartments, too. Mine has two bedrooms. Plenty of room for two old war horses to hobble around. You hear me, dear Helen?"

Helen shook her head. "I hear you Essie Mae, but I'm not listening. Sapphire Island has plenty of room for a couple of old war horses to 'hobble around' as you so caustically put it."

Sam raised his dark eyes to the sky in exasperation, though a grin tugged at the corners of his full mouth. It was obvious he was accustomed to the two women skirmishing, and found it amusing.

Ignoring her hostesses' bantering for the moment and barely able to contain her joy at being there, Susan breathed in the scent of the island, the tang of salt air mingling with the sweet scent of flowers. She suddenly heard Sam say, "Miss Helen, Mr. Kaleb will be waiting."

"So he will." Helen nodded with a sigh, looking slightly apologetic. Eyeing Essie's raised brow, she added, "He arrived last week. Surprised me, to say the least. I didn't expect to see him again until Christmas. Lord knows why he's here. Says he's doing research for a new book, but you know Kaleb."

"Yes, I know Kaleb," Essie said a bit wistfully. "He's a carbon copy of his father and uncle, dear Helen. Here today, gone tomorrow. I think the Knight men had a streak of the old wanderlust in their blood. Only seems right Kaleb should follow along, eh?"

Their comments stirred Susan's drifting thoughts into a frenzy of activity, and she was suddenly filled with questions she was hesitant to ask. Kaleb was

Helen Knight's son, so why hadn't he been a part of the welcoming committee? Essie was his aunt, after all. And why had Sam's words sounded so urgent? Why had Helen sounded so apologetic? The picture conjured up was one of a man who thought he was king, and who impatiently waited for his court. Susan decided she disliked Kaleb Knight without having the pleasure—or displeasure—of meeting him.

Minutes later the house came into view, and Susan gasped. It stood against a shelter of trees, cool and inviting. A veranda ran along the width, supporting massive vines bearing purple, yellow, and white blossoms. "It's beautiful!" Susan exclaimed. "Did your husband build it?"

Helen shook her head. "Kade built the original house, but, oh, dear, that was a far cry from what's standing now. This masterpiece was my son's idea. It took one summer and a few weeks to build, and when it was finally completed, he was satisfied it would meet our needs. Though between you and me, it never was meant for anything but his own needs. It's a bit too large for my taste. One thing Kaleb made sure of, my dear, and that's comfort. The house is well equipped. Once a week, supplies are flown in from Samoa, and the villagers supply milk and chickens. Fruit comes right off the trees, and down near the pond, a small vegetable garden thrives year-round, thanks to Sam and his expertise."

"The garden takes on its healthy glow from Laelia's loving touch as well, Miss Helen," Sam ventured modestly.

"Laelia is my little housekeeper and companion," Helen said, nodding in agreement. "Sam and Laelia are from the village, though they stay here during the week. I'm sure you'll enjoy visiting a true Samoan village, Susan."

"Never could get the hang of their strange housing and customs," Essie retorted with a flip of her gray head. "The people are a delightful lot, but I like my windows to contain glass, my door to have locks, and my floors to be made of wood instead of crushed coral. Sam knows how I feel, eh, Sam?"

Sam didn't appear offended, and with a nod said, "Many people have difficulty accepting our way of life, but still, there are those who come and want to stay."

Susan could see it wasn't going to be an easy task to convince Helen to move back to the States. This magnificent island was her home, and she truly loved it. Strangely enough, Susan understood. Already, she had the feeling she could easily become one of Sam's "there are those who come and want to stay." She truly hoped she could become one with the island, as Sam had put it.

A young woman stepped onto the veranda. "It's good to see you again Laelia," Essie greeted her, giving the girl a hug. "My, but you get prettier every day! I'd like you to meet Susan McRay, my friend, neighbor, and traveling companion."

"Talofa, Miss Susan," Laelia smiled, bowing her head coyly. Her lovely almond-shaped eyes were friendly and curious. She wore a pale blue sarong— a puletasi. It fit the girl to perfection, showing off every curve of her lithe figure.

"I hope to wear a puletasi while I'm here," Susan said, "but I can't imagine looking as pretty in one as you do."

"Well, now, I think you two girls are going to get

along famously," Helen chuckled, leading the way into the house. And then of Laelia, she asked, "Where's Kaleb?"

"Right here, Mother."

Susan turned as Kaleb Knight strode through a door off the living room. Her first thought—after her heart had stopped skipping about and she could catch her breath—was that there must be some mistake. This giant of a man, whose russet hair and full beard framed his face like a bush, and whose dark green eyes pierced through her, skewering her to the spot where she stood, couldn't be Kaleb Knight! He wore faded blue jeans and a sleeveless gray sweatshirt; had she met him on a San Francisco street corner, she would have dismissed him as a fisherman just off the boat, or a down-on-his-luck bum. Either way, she wouldn't have given him the time of day. Worse, he was so out of sync with this beautiful island that she felt offended, literally assaulted.

Authority was written all over him, however, and although Susan suddenly had the uncontrollable urge to get as far away from him as possible, she pushed it aside as ridiculous. After all, he *was* Kaleb Knight, and this was *his* island.

"This is my son, Kaleb," Helen said, making introductions quickly, almost apologetically, seeming to sense Susan's discomfort. "Kaleb, dear, this is Aunt Essie's friend Susan McRay." She broke off, biting her lip in obvious frustration.

Kaleb gave Susan a brief nod while his insolent green eyes coolly took inventory, sliding from her hair on down until they came to rest on the polished toenails poking out of her sandals.

Susan, in turn, studied him. His nose was straight

and strong, his eyes a most disconcerting green, and, even though she had to admit his sun-bronzed body, with muscles and bulges in just the right places, was the epitome of virility, he was clearly the arrogant, barbaric type. She found herself disliking him even more than when she'd pictured him as the man who would be king.

She looked up to find him watching her. He acknowledged her assessment with a lift of his arched brow. She flushed, returning his nod with a perfunctory one of her own. It was then she noticed Essie's tightly drawn, disapproving mouth.

"The least you could do was shave and put on some decent clothing," Essie grumbled up at him.

"If I shaved, I'd scare off my pets," Kaleb responded, directing a lopsided grin in his aunt's general direction.

Two elongated dimples had creased his cheeks, and Susan found herself drawn to them—and to his beautiful even teeth, which appeared whiter than white against his craggy, tanned face. She looked away quickly, reminding herself that his negative qualities far outweighed any that might be considered positive.

"Seems to me your pets would be frightened off by the sight of you now, young man," Essie muttered, shaking her head with dismay. "I declare, you grow more and more like your father and Uncle Carl every day! There was a streak of stubbornness in the Knight men a mile wide. I suppose you shouldn't be any different. I've always envied your mother because she has a son to carry on, but I can also sympathize with the traumas she must face because of it."

At the mention of his pets, Susan felt a prickle down her back, imagining King Kaleb and his pit full of crocodiles. The thought was pointless and silly and she shrugged it off. She had far too many lovely sights to focus her attention on to allow herself even a shred of apprehension.

For one thing, the room they were in was the most beautiful she had ever seen. Sunlight, cast from shuttered windows thrown open to the morning breeze, shimmered and danced across the polished floor. A ceiling fan hummed above a long, white sofa and matching chairs, and cane lamps graced hand-carved tables. Pillows of all shapes and sizes and bearing the colors of the island were tossed at random. Flower-filled tubs and baskets gave the room the look and feel of a greenhouse. The heady scent of rich earth, Gardenia, frangipani, Hibiscus, and White Ginger transported Susan into a valley of dreams. How wonderful it would be to live in such luxury in the middle of paradise.

"Well, I can see you appreciate beauty," Helen laughed merrily, noting Susan's delighted expression. "You'll love the rest of the house, too, Susan, but first, you'll want to freshen up after your long journey. Laelia will show you to the guest cottage. Essie always shares my quarters when she visits, so don't panic when you find yourself transported into another world and feel all alone. You'll have a phone with a direct hookup to the main house. Another of Kaleb's innovations.

"Please don't feel we are ostracizing you from the hub of things, honey. It's simply a matter of necessity. Although this house is large, it lacks bedroom space, and inasmuch as you're young and adventuresome, we thought you wouldn't mind the cottage . . . might even enjoy it."

Kaleb was across the room talking to Laelia, and Helen lowered her voice. "Kaleb designed the cottage for his own personal use, actually, and usually stays there when he's home, but since . . . well, no matter. Laelia will show you the way, and we'll meet in the south garden in an hour."

Susan followed Laelia, grateful for the opportunity to escape. The thought of a soothing bath and a few moments alone appealed to her immensely, but more than that, she needed time to sort out her whirling thoughts.

"Don't panic when you find yourself transported into another world." What on earth had Helen meant by that remark? And what had she started to say about her son? Why wasn't he staying at the cottage? Not that Susan objected to staying apart from the main house. On the contrary, she rather liked the idea, but she couldn't help but feel there was some sort of a mystery afoot.

CHAPTER
Two

LAELIA LED THE way across a plush, palm-fringed lawn to a path winding through a jungle of dense vegetation filled with the sounds of chattering birds. Jade-green ferns and crimson Anthurium grew in profusion along the path, and overhead masses of breathtaking orchids spilled in tangled confusion. Susan's excitement mounted to a fevered pitch with every new turn in the path. Not even in her wildest dreams could she have imagined such exquisite beauty.

When they reached the clearing, and Susan gasped with delight, Laelia laughed. "It is a beautiful place," she said. "One of the many pleasures on our island."

There were no words to describe the spectacular setting that had suddenly unfolded before her. Susan

stood in awe, barely able to catch her breath, afraid
that one slight movement in any direction might dis-
solve the magic of the moment. "That can't be the
cottage," she whispered.

Laelia smiled and nodded. "I think it is what is
called a house in the trees."

The tree house stood beside a picturesque lagoon,
snuggled within the protective branches of a gnarled
banyan tree. "Oh, it's beautiful!" Susan exclaimed.
"Is there a ladder or some sort of access?"

"There are steps on the back side of the tree,"
Laelia replied, breaking into a trot to keep up with
Susan, who easily found the steps. They had been
carved into the deeply slanted section of trunk. With
the aid of wooden pegs that served as handles, she
effortlessly maneuvered the climb.

Laelia's eyes were bright when she joined Susan
in the foyer. "You like your place to stay?" she asked
eagerly.

"Like it? Oh, Laelia, I love it! I can't imagine Mr.
Knight giving this up for the comforts of the main
house."

Laelia lowered her eyes as a smile played at the
corners of her pretty mouth. "Perhaps you will also
want to stay in the big house after you spend a night
alone. Those who are not accustomed to island sounds
sometimes become frightened."

"I could never feel frightened in a beautiful place
like this," Susan responded dreamily, feasting her
eyes on her new surroundings.

The living room was cool and clean. To accentuate
the air of freshness, it was decorated with light, polished woods and tropical prints in pale aquamarine.
Woven mats graced the floor, and the shuttered, glass-

less windows, like those in the main house, were thrown open to the gentle morning breeze. Artifacts, touches of Samoa, completed the picture of serene simplicity.

Apparently pleased with Susan's reaction, Laelia led the way to the bedroom and attached bath, standing aside while Susan whirled about with excitement. Everything, from the elaborately carved oversized bed with its aquamarine velvet spread, to the white marbled bathroom, drew gasps and praise from her.

"The bed was hand carved by my uncle Mutu," Laelia volunteered. "He is a good craftsman, and some of his work is sent by ship to Pago Pago."

"Your uncle does beautiful work," Susan said, gently running her hand over the intricate design. "Are the artifacts—the mats, statues, bowls, and baskets—from your village, too?"

"Yes," Laelia replied. "My uncle carved the table in the kitchen as well." She broke off, smiling at Susan's wide-eyed expression. "There is a veranda beyond the door to your right. It leads to the kitchen."

There, Susan found not only the lovely carved teakwood table and chairs, but also well-stocked cupboards and a small refrigerator. Stepping out onto the veranda, she sighed with contentment. Below, like a whispered song, the sleepy lagoon lapped against pink-tinged sand.

Her thoughts drifted to the man who had made all this possible, the man she had disliked since stepping on the pier. She had visualized Kaleb Knight as a king among those he considered fools, not the kind of man who would build his castle in a tree with such obvious thought and consideration. Had she been wrong in her preconceived judgment?

"The magic of the island is in your eyes, Miss Susan," Laelia said softly. "There is much on our island that is beautiful, and you will see it all in good time, but now, you must ready yourself. Miss Helen and Miss Essie will be waiting in the south garden."

"And Mr. Knight. Will he be there, too?" Susan asked cautiously.

Laelia's brown eyes held a hint of amusement as she replied, "Mr. Kaleb will be there. Shall I unpack your things?"

It was apparent Laelia wasn't going to venture even a shred of information about Kaleb Knight without prodding, and Susan didn't want to appear overly interested or curious. She hoped time and patience would bring her the answers to her puzzling questions. "Yes, please unpack, Laelia," she said, "and you might like to pick out something for me to wear."

"Choosing from your American clothes would be fun, but not necessary, Miss Susan. I think you will want to wear a puletasi. Miss Helen had several of them made up when she learned of your arrival. You will find them hanging in the bedroom closet."

Susan was pleased, though not surprised. Nothing more could possibly surprise her on this verdant, magical island.

A little less than an hour later Susan and Laelia made their way along the path to the main house. When they reached the velvet lawn, Laelia turned away from the house, following a path through a small grove of orange trees.

"Oranges?" Susan queried, marveling over the deep-colored fruit hanging like ornaments on a Christmas tree. Their pungent aroma filled the air. "Oranges bring to mind California or Florida, but certainly not a South Pacific island."

"Mr. Kade planted many trees when he and Miss Helen first came to the island," Laelia said. "Orange, lemon, pear, and apple. He always said they were his memories of home." She paused, giving Susan an impish smile. "You look very beautiful, Miss Susan. That color becomes you."

Her compliment was unexpected, and Susan flushed with pleasure. "Thank you," she said, warmed by the girl's thoughtfulness. "I feel different, that's for sure."

Actually, she felt beautiful. The bath had been wonderfully refreshing, but the real thrill had come when she'd slipped into the soft tangerine and white print puletasi. Instantly, she had been transformed into an island maiden. To complete the picture, she wore sandals (unable to bring herself to go barefoot), and a creamy-white Gardenia in her chestnut hair.

They had reached the edge of the orange grove, and stepping out onto a smaller, more secluded lawn, they entered a Japanese garden, complete with fish pond, pagoda, a wooden bridge, and a little teahouse open to the blue Pacific. Helen and Essie were sitting in the teahouse, and when they saw the women emerging from the trees, they waved a welcome.

"Ah, there you are!" Helen called out as the girls approached. "Oh, Essie Mae, look at Susan. Doesn't she look lovely?"

"Beautiful," Essie agreed, bobbing her gray head. "I must say, Susan certainly looks better than you do in those long thingamabobs!"

"We'll soon have sweet rolls and fresh fruit to nibble on with our tea," Helen offered, ignoring Essie's remark, "but I think we'll wait until Kaleb joins us. That's my way of getting him to eat. Sit down, my dear, and tell me how you like the cottage."

Before Susan could respond, Kaleb suddenly appeared, looking more menacing than she remembered. "It's not a cottage, Mother, it's a tree house," he said sharply.

"Oh, come, Kaleb," Helen snorted. "Calling it a tree house sounds so . . . so childish!"

"But it *is* a tree house," he replied curtly. Once again, Susan felt her heart flutter.

Essie shook her gray head. "You had plenty of time to change clothes and shave, my dear nephew. I declare you grow more stubborn with every birthday. Thirty-three years old and you'd might as well be eighteen. Susan is only twenty-five, and I'll bet she could teach you a thing or two!"

"I'll bet she could," Kaleb drawled as his casual glance flickered over Susan's face. "But the fact remains, if I shave, my pets will think I'm a stranger."

He was teasing his aunt, and she tapped her foot and pursed her lips. "Well, call your pets then so Susan can see what all the fuss is about, eh?"

At the mention of his pets, the crocodile pit came to Susan's mind, though now even a hole full of crocodiles seemed rather tame. Not knowing what to expect, she held her breath while Kaleb gave a soft, lilting whistle. Immediately, three beautiful birds descended upon them, landing on his outstretched arm. Susan exhaled a sigh of relief.

"Meet Tasi, Pula, and Moana," Kaleb announced, dimples creasing his cheeks.

The velvety pale-green birds were happily preening their feathers and shaking their heads. They lifted their topknots in a display of utmost vanity, and from their

throats came soft chirps, chatters, and warbles. For-
getting about the man who held them, Susan exclaimed with pleasure. "How can you tell them apart?
They look like triplets!"

Helen spoke for her son with pride lighting up her
eyes. "Kaleb has a way with the birds on our island,
Susan. Even when he was a youngster, he managed
to tame them so they would follow him about. Surprisingly enough, he could always tell one from the
other. He still can. When he's Stateside tending to
business, they truly miss him."

"These beauties are called torquoisine parrakeets,"
Kaleb interjected. "They're just one of over fifty species of our fair-feathered friends on the island. The
torquoisine nest in the rocks at the north end of the
island." He was watching Susan with veiled, unreadable eyes.

Feeling a bit flustered, Susan asked, "May I hold
one?"

Kaleb stood up and requested Susan to do the same.
Gently, he transferred one of the birds to her hand.
"You're holding Tasi," he told her. "If you'll notice,
she has a small blue circle beside her beak."

"Oh, you beautiful baby," Susan murmured softly,
reaching out with her free hand to stroke its soft head.
The bird fluffed its feathers and cocked its head, looking up at her with round, curious eyes. "Tasi, beautiful
Tasi," Susan cooed. "You're as beautiful as the island
around you."

"I declare, will you just look at the way that bird
has taken to Susan," Essie chuckled. "Better watch
out, my dear nephew. Susan's apt to steal your thunder, eh?"

Susan's cheeks flushed as she raised her eyes to

the strange man standing beside her. How could he, by his very appearance, be such a blight on the island yet so much a part of it? Realizing she was a silly romantic, that visions of tropical paradise inhabited by beautiful natives and a handsome, sun-kissed stranger in a white suit who was the master of it all, belonged in the movies, her flush deepened.

"Thank you for sharing your pets with me," she said with a guilty rush of warmth in her voice. "They are truly as beautiful as the island. You have a gift for taming them and should be very proud."

"I am, and I'm glad you're pleased." He smiled down at her. "Perhaps you'd like to see where they nest." As he spoke, green jungle fire played in the depths of his eyes. "It's a dangerous walk I'm afraid, since the north end of the island is a far cry from what you see here, but if you're the adventuresome sort—"

"I think she must be," Helen interrupted. "Otherwise, she'd be screaming at me now for sticking her in that desolate cottage." To Susan, she added, "You never did tell us how you like it, my dear. If you don't think you'll be able to handle it, don't be afraid to speak up. You can always exchange sleeping quarters with Kaleb. That should have been the arrangement anyway. I'm afraid my son has yet to learn that life consists of compromise..."

Kaleb looked so exasperated with his mother that Susan stifled a giggle. "On the contrary, Mrs. Knight," she said, "the tree house is a dream. I adore it and look forward to calling it home for the next three weeks." Her soft, violet eyes fluttered to Kaleb's craggy face once again. "Frankly, though, I don't understand why you prefer the main house, Mr.

Knight. I understand you're a writer, and I would think the solitude of the tree house would give you a wealth of inspiration."

Helen cleared her throat, Essie coughed, and Laelia, who was fussing with the table of food, shook her head in dismay. Susan's heart thumped. Realizing that the tree house must hold some horrid, unwanted memory for Kaleb Knight, she handed him the bird and stepped back. "I'm truly sorry if I offended you. I just thought..."

"It's true Kaleb is a writer," Helen quickly interjected, darting a pleading glance at her son. "He writes South Sea adventure novels when he isn't tending to the family silver mine in Arizona. But as for the tree house giving him inspiration..."

Kaleb's eyes blazed like hot emeralds. "If the story must be told, I'd rather tell it myself." With a snap of his fingers the birds flew off into the trees. Then without moving, he said, "It's true I'm a writer, but I doubt the tree house would give me inspiration. I was engaged to be married. I built the tree house...well, it was to be our home. Needless to say, my fiancée did not like the thought of moving to a remote island in the South Pacific and living in a tree house. Later, I found out the thought of marriage repulsed her, too. End of story. But it's not the end of the world, as my mother and aunt would have you believe. I've learned to live with it. I'd prefer to tear down the cottage instead of leaving it there as a constant reminder that love is life's lousiest dilemma, but mother insisted we keep it as a guest house. She was correct as usual. I'm glad you like it and are comfortable. At least it hasn't been a total waste."

With a sigh, Susan tried to swallow the cottony

lump in her throat. She didn't know why his confession had touched her, but it had. She ached for him, knowing the pain he must have endured, and supposed it was because she herself had just experienced a broken romance, and because after only a few hours on the island she was held totally captive. She could imagine the heart-felt jolt of knowing he could never share its beauty with the woman he loved.

"I'm glad you didn't tear it down," she said finally, finding her voice in the depths of her own despair. "It's an absolutely marvelous structure, and I think it will be therapeutic for me. I broke my engagement just a few weeks ago and need a place where I can put my thoughts in order. Your aunt was wonderful to make my escape possible."

"Aunt Essie is a terrific lady," Kaleb agreed with dimples flashing. "Shall we forget about the past and see what the immediate future holds?"

"The immediate future holds cups of jasmine tea, sweet rolls, and fresh fruit," Helen announced with a look of relief as Laelia appeared with the food. Helen smiled at Susan. "You'll find the tree house well-stocked with provisions, my dear, and, although you're free to use as much of it as you want, we'd like you to take your meals in the main house. This is your vacation, and you shouldn't have to cook."

"If this is any indication of what I can expect," Susan said, munching on a sweet roll, "I'd be foolish to refuse your offer." The roll melted in her mouth, the tea was hot, and oh, the fruit! There were strawberries as large as lemons, sweet orange sections dipped in powdered sugar, slices of succulent pineapple, and chunks of rosy melon. She couldn't stand on the ceremony of daintily picking at her food. She was famished, and ate accordingly, noting that Kaleb was doing the same.

"It does my old heart good to see the youngsters eat like they're really enjoying it," Essie said between sips of tea. "I suspect Kaleb has been on a food strike like Susan. Nothing worse for the digestion than a broken romance. Well, it looks to me as though we might be able to get them both on the road to recovery, eh, dear Helen?"

"Or the island will," Helen reasoned with her green eyes aglow. "Susan was right when she said the tree house will be therapeutic. Everything on our island seems to make folks forget their problems."

"Do you get the impression they're ganging up on us?" Kaleb asked with a wry grin.

Susan nodded. "But it's a good feeling, knowing someone cares."

Helen cleared her throat. "I understand your father lives in Los Angeles, Susan."

"At the present time. He's in construction and moves around a lot. When my mother was alive, things were a little more stable."

"And you're an only child?"

"Yes. Essie has made up for my lack of family ties, though. She's been every family member all rolled into one. Even more, she's been my friend."

Essie's eyes filled with tears, and she hurriedly brushed them away. "Susan has been all things to me too. She's been the daughter I never had. Well, enough of this! I think it's time Susan had a look around the island. What do you think, Helen? Perhaps we could call on Sam."

"Sam is working in the garden," Kaleb interrupted, unwinding his sinewy frame from the chair. "If Susan wants to see the island, I'll be happy to give her a tour." He extended his hand and helped her to her feet. "Though I don't think we should do it all today. The island is bigger than it looks. I suggest we cover the immediate area now, and then tomorrow after we have an early breakfast—and dress for the trek—we can extend our tour on horseback."

"Horseback?" Susan gasped in astonishment.

"It's the only satisfactory means of covering a long distance." He still held her hand, and his brows arched above his jade-green eyes. "You can ride, can't you?"

Irritated, Susan removed her hand from his. He seemed to be laughing at her, though she couldn't be sure; his beard covered so much of his expression. Only his eyes lay open and vulnerable to be read, and now they too were shielded from her scrutiny. "Yes, I can ride, Mr. Knight," she finally managed to reply. "I'm just surprised you have horses on the island, that's all, though I guess I should know better by now. Surprises seem to go with the territory, popping off trees as easily as coconuts . . ."

CHAPTER
Three

"YOU SOUND AS though every minute since stepping off the seaplane has been filled with surprises," Kaleb said, taking her arm to steady her as they climbed over a tangle of vines. "Care to elaborate?"

They were walking along a pathway toward the beach, and Susan stopped, reaching out to touch the delicate petals of a pink Hibiscus. "For one thing, I wasn't prepared for this breathtaking beauty," she said. "It's paradise beyond my wildest dreams. The flowers and different shades of green . . . I paint with oils in my spare time, you see. I'm a starving artist who supports herself teaching art, so I suppose I'm seeing it as an exciting challenge. Mixing just the right colors and then trying to capture it all . . ."

When she drew no response, she went on. "From the air, the island resembled an emerald tapestry, resting against turquoise velvet, and now that I'm actually here and a part of it all, it's even more spectacular than I imagined. Essie told me it would capture my heart, and it has—"

She broke off, stealing a glance at his rugged profile. Did he think she was a silly little romantic for spouting such flowery words? Whatever he thought, he gave no indication, keeping his eyes on the path.

"And Sam and Laelia," she continued quickly, trying to cover her uneasiness. "They're so friendly. I was surprised they speak such fluent English. I don't know what I expected—" She broke off again, biting her lip. What was there about Kaleb Knight that so unnerved her?

"The people of Samoa are among the friendliest anywhere," Kaleb said, his voice lifting with pride. "And most can speak English. When my parents came to the island thirty-four years ago, they found a culture like no other. The people, though determined to preserve their grace and dignity, were eager to learn the ways and language of the Western world. Most could speak Pidgin English, and, since experimental educational TV began in Pago Pago and the community college was founded in Tutuila, English has become a universal language. Their own language hasn't been forgotten, however, nor have they destroyed their beautiful, extraordinarily persistent culture." He paused, deep in thought.

"Please go on," said Susan. "It's fascinating."

Kaleb glanced at her briefly and continued. "Sam and Laelia's fluent vocabulary is the direct result of my parents' efforts. My father in particular. He was a good teacher, and a good friend. He brought a lot more to the village than language. He taught them about agriculture and how to better their life-style without changing it. In return, we learned about their simple, though elegant, way of life, and achieved inner peace and happiness because of it."

Enchanted by Kaleb's colorful accounting, and surrounded with an aura of wonder, Susan found her voice husky when she asked, "Were you born on the island?"

"Yes, I was." He was looking at her now, his eyes green slits penetrating through dusky, copperish lashes. "It's a long story. Are you sure you're interested?"

"Oh, yes," she exclaimed, eager to hear whatever he might want to tell her.

They had reached the beach, and Kaleb pointed to the left, away from the pier where the seaplane had landed. "There's a stretch of beach around the bend you might be interested in, if you feel up to walking that far."

Susan nodded and slipped off her sandals. She followed Kaleb's tracks in the powdery white sand, the bulk of him blotting out the sun. She couldn't see his face, but she could sense his withdrawl, the feeling that he was alone with his thoughts. Had he changed his mind and no longer wanted to share the past with her? Had she said something to offend him? Other thoughts whirled as she struggled to keep pace. Who was the woman who had captured his heart? What would he look like without the beard?

They came to a grove of date palms jutting out into the sand, the center of which looked like the Garden of Eden. "We'll stop here and rest," he announced casually. "You can drink from the spring. The water is fresh."

The spring bubbled up and over colorful rocks before emptying into a crystal pool. Susan dropped to her knees on the mossy bank. "It's happening again," she sighed. "Just when I think I've seen everything, something else comes along."

"And it will seem that way until the last stone is turned, if you'll forgive the platitude," Kaleb said, sitting down with his back against a palm tree. "Unfortunately, you won't be around long enough. In my thirty-three years, I've yet to find the last stone. Each morning brings a new delight. A fresh blossom, an unusual leaf, an unknown strain of migrating bird, a beautiful shell on the beach, a newborn baby in the village. Even the sand changes with time. A tropical storm will change a running stream and uncover other wonders for investigation. A lifetime wouldn't be long enough to discover all there is to see."

He was in the shade, and, although she couldn't see his eyes, she could feel the molten probing of luminous green sparks. She had never met a man like Kaleb Knight, nor was she likely to again. He stood alone; a subtle mixture of strength, arrogance, and sensitivity. Would it ever be possible to truly know and understand him? She took a deep breath. Now, more than ever, she was curious about his past.

"I—If you'd rather not tell me about your childhood..."

Dimples creased and white teeth flashed. "So you haven't forgotten. Not that I mind telling you. It's just a very long story. You've only got three weeks..." The dimples deepened. "Well, maybe I can simplify it.

"My parents married in 1946, just after the war. As a wedding gift, my grandfather gave them a round-trip ticket to the Samoas. They fell in love with the islands and stayed, against my grandfather's wishes. He'd hoped my father, the eldest of two sons, would carry on with the family mining business, but his coaxing settled on deaf ears. It's not clear how they decided on this particular island. Mother claims Father chose it for its accessibility to Pago Pago, and Father, as I recall, claimed it was Mother's choice because she fell in love with the sapphire water surrounding it. It doesn't matter. The fact is, they lived and loved in paradise..." His expressive eyes seemed to ask: *Are you sure you want me to continue with this?*

"Please go on," Susan encouraged. "I want to hear all about the Knight family saga."

"Two years later, Uncle Carl, who was a prominent San Francisco attorney, married Aunt Essie. That same summer, I was born. I grew up playing with the Samoan kids, even thinking I was one of them, while Grandfather was on the verge of disowning us all. He was convinced we were spawned by the devil. Uncle Carl refused to become part of the mining operation and my father had already washed his hands of it. His profession lay clearly in the field of education. But Grandfather was convinced Father had made a home for his wife and son on an island of pagans. That wasn't true, of course, the Samoan people being a highly religious race, but convincing Grandfather was another story.

"Father tutored me until I was eight, and then, to keep peace with Grandfather, and possibly because he felt I needed more exposure to the outside world, he sent me to Arizona to live. Grandfather saw me through school and college, where I majored in education and minored in journalism. I wanted to follow in my father's footsteps as a teacher or become a writer or both. Unfortunately, I've had barely enough time to write, let alone teach.

"Grandfather took sick while I was working on my M.A., and when he realized the end was near, informed me he was leaving the mining operation in my hands. I was the only one he could trust to continue with his life's work. I looked at the old man who was withering away before my eyes, and knew there was no way I could tell him how I really felt. That was eight years ago, and I've been trapped ever since.

"I would much prefer a classroom full of smiling faces, or the beauty of Sapphire Island, to the desolate acres of Arizona. Fortunately, I have a good crew and can leave on occasion without worry. That wasn't what my grandfather had in mind, but I can't bring myself to be totally dedicated. Guilt rides heavily on my shoulders, especially now, because I'm the only one left to carry on."

Feeling shaky after listening to Kaleb's honest, open words, Susan shook her head. "I think you're foolish to feel guilty. You've done what was expected of you."

"Maybe, but it's hard to forget Grandfather's unhappiness. My grandmother died before their twentieth anniversary, and then all his sons left to go their own way. All he ever really wanted was to have his family around him and to make the mining operation a continued success, carried on in the family tradition. He was a proud man, and mining was his life."

Kaleb stood up and stretched from side to side as

though to rid himself of his guilt as well as the kinks in his body. Susan understood why he felt as he did, but he was wrong, so very wrong. "But it wasn't your father's life or your uncle's life, Mr. Knight. That was their choice. Shouldn't you have that same choice? Traditions are made to be broken or started anew. No man should be made a prisoner because of them. Life is too short to live it halfway."

She had moved to his side and reached out to touch his arm. "Someday, you'll have a son of your own, and what will you do then? Will you carry on your grandfather's wishes through him? Perhaps he'll like running the silver mine in Arizona. Perhaps he'll fall in love with your island paradise. Perhaps he'll want to share them both as you're doing now, or pursue something totally different. The important point is that he should have the chance to decide without being made to feel sad or guilty."

She gulped in air, feeling as though her next breath might be her last. She had no right to dictate what he should or shouldn't do with his life. What had possessed her? She'd been caught up in his private misery, and now she was open and vulnerable to any attack he might make.

Kaleb's green eyes became dark, swampy pools as he scowled down at her. When he spoke, it was with the coldness of a winter day. "There will be no son. I don't ever intend to marry—and I certainly won't fall in love again. Only blind fools fall in love." His eyes softened at her stricken expression. "But thank you for caring. You're a very perceptive young lady with a heart as large as your magnificent violet eyes. By the way, my friends call me Kaleb."

She searched his face, but could detect no malice or hostility, and the tension she'd felt drained away. He was offering friendship, and she couldn't think of anything she'd like better. "All right, Kaleb," she said, giving him a shadowy smile. "Thank you for sharing your life with me."

She moved to a rock beside the pool and sat down, dangling her toes in the cool water.

Had he seen the sadness in her eyes before she turned away? She understood the pain of a broken heart. She felt the same stabbing ache and probably would for a long time to come. But she couldn't imagine wanting to go through life empty and alone because of one shattering experience. Everyone deserved a second chance at love.

"Now it's your turn, young lady," Kaleb intoned, joining her on the rock. Sunlight glinted through his russet hair, and his eyes twinkled. "Turnabout is fair play. I want to hear all about the McRay family."

Susan found herself flushing. Was it because of Kaleb's interest? Or because his muscular thigh rested against her own, stirring an awareness she had thought lay buried under her battered heart? "I'm afraid the story of my life, by comparison, will be just a bore."

"I'll be the judge of that. I know you live in San Francisco and rent an apartment from my aunt. The two of you have become good friends. Your mother died years ago and your father lives in Los Angeles. You're an only child and were engaged to be married until quite recently. You like to paint in your spare time. What do you do when you're not painting?"

"Paint." Susan smiled. "I'm an art instructor at Art International in San Francisco. It's an art supply store with a studio in the rear for classes. I have a good following with more students signing up all the time. My technique is a little different than most artists since I use a wash of oil and come up with a finished painting reminiscent of water colors." A delicate pink tinged her cheeks. "Don't get me started or I'll end up boring you with every detail."

"Art in any form could never be boring," Kaleb drawled in a comfortable, lazy tone. "And so you paint morning, noon, and night. What do you do when you need to get away from the smell of turpentine?"

"I like to swim, dance, hike, and ski. I met Paul at a party in Squaw Valley." She broke off, feeling her throat constrict.

"Ah," said Kaleb. "A well-rounded, adventure-some young lady meets the man of her dreams at a party and it's love at first sight. The snowy mountain, the glamorous lodge, and the crystal-clear nights add to the moment. Only when they come back to earth, the magic is replaced by reality. In the city, on a street corner, in a supermarket, things look different. Perhaps he resents her dedication to her career. Whatever, the dream becomes a nightmare."

His eyes bore into her, unblinking, the green of the jungle penetrating the violet mists of early morning. Not only was he the most unnerving man she'd ever met, he was also the most aggravating. She whirled on him angrily. "How can you be so quick to judge? You know nothing about Paul and virtually nothing about me! The problems I had with Paul weren't because of my work or conflicting views."

He shrugged impatiently. "What then? What did this Paul person do to you to make you want to travel to the ends of the earth to lick your wounds?"

For a moment, Susan felt smothered, unable to breathe. Why was he asking these questions? Why was he intent on ruining a perfectly beautiful day with his bothersome prying? She'd traveled to the "ends of the earth," as he'd put it, to try and forget Paul Shelley. How could she succeed if at every turn she was reminded of him? "If you're working on a plot for a new book, forget it," she snapped.

He took in the angry flush of her cheeks and drew a deep breath. "I'm sorry, Susan," he apologized. "I didn't mean to upset you." Dimples flashed as his lips pulled across the brilliant whiteness of his teeth. "Forgive me?"

His appealing smile melted her heart. "If you'll forgive me for being so defensive." She looked into the depths of his eyes, noticing for the first time minute flecks of amber and gold. "I—I loved him, and I thought he loved me. All I wanted was honesty. He was seeing other women nearly the entire time we were engaged. I know there are men like that . . . men who need the freedom an affair can bring. He actually expected me to understand. The night I caught him red-handed, he tried to tell me it had nothing to do with us, with how much he loved me. He needed me and why couldn't I be open-minded? He told me to climb out of the dark ages and join reality." She looked away, unable to meet the kindness and understanding in Kaleb's clear eyes.

He stood up, reaching for her hand. "I think it's time we moved on. The beach I mentioned earlier isn't far, and then Mother will be expecting us for lunch."

She was instantly aware of the strength of his touch as he took her hand and they walked down the beach. The sun was high now. Stepping from the coolness of the little oasis onto the vast expanse of beach took her breath away. The sand was hot on her bare feet, and she danced a little jig.

"It will be cooler along the water's edge, my tei-netiti," Kaleb chuckled. "Just don't step on a shell or a chunk of coral."

She couldn't imagine what "teinetiti" meant, but was hesitant to ask.

They walked to where the water foamed against the white-washed sand. He hadn't released her hand, and she'd become conscious of his long, sinewy fingers entangled with her own.

"It's just ahead. See where the sand grows pink?"

Susan nodded, enraptured by the spectacular sight. The pinkish sand, much like the sand near the tree house, was the product of thousands of crushed shells and pink coral ground into a powdery brilliance that almost blinded her. In several places, large rocks overhung the beach, and in between spilled tropical foliage, a waterfall of pink, purple, and white orchids. In the coral outcroppings pools of glassy water glistened in the sunlight.

"I thought you might appreciate it," Kaleb said, winking at her. "You can add it to your list of surprises."

"I can't believe there are so many different shells!" she exclaimed, hurrying from one to the next. "Do you know the names of them all?" She listened while Kaleb rattled off leopard, cone, tooth, and bubble shells. When he had completed the list, adding the names of all the colorful fish that darted about in the shallows, she shook her head. "An artist's brush couldn't do it justice."

"Though I suppose you'll try?" he asked, watching her intently.

"Yes, I'll try. Do you use your gorgeous island as a background for your books?"

"As a writer, I couldn't bypass all this natural beauty any more than you could walk away without attempting to capture it on canvas. I've had two books published, and both are set in the Samoas. The next ten will more than likely be as well. I doubt I'll ever run out of living, breathing, vibrant description. I'm more apt to run out of time. A book paints a picture as well as an artist's brush. Perhaps my next heroine will have hair the color of mountain honey and violet eyes."

Susan's eyes grew wide. "You write romantic novels?"

"No. I write tales of adventure in paradise, though there is always a hero and heroine . . . and love."

He stood so close, Susan could feel the warmth of him, could see the haunted longing in his eyes. With infinite slowness, his face lowered. She knew he was going to kiss her and she was powerless to stop him. When his mouth finally closed over hers, she was totally unprepared for the devastating jolt to her senses. Her lips parted, accepting the deep probings of his tongue as a moan escaped from her throat. Not so long ago, she had experienced a romance that had known no boundaries, but even in those most passionate moments, she had never felt like this! Her body was aglow with the pleasure of his touch. She pressed more intimately against him.

When he released her, his breath was warm on her cheek, the breath of a man who held her as gently and lovingly as he might hold one of his fragile birds.

"The pleasure of a beautiful woman's kiss," he said softly, kissing the tip of her nose, "is one of life's pure delights. Are you ready to go back to the house?"

"In a few moments," Susan said shakily. "It's so beautiful here. I wish I could stay forever."

His eyes flickered, green jade darkening to onyx. "Do you mean on the island?"

"N-no. I mean here, on this stretch of beach."

He smiled, taking her hand in his. "But nothing lasts forever, my little romantic friend. Nothing."

On the contrary, she knew one thing would, if no other. The exquisite feel of his warm, sensually demanding lips on her own.

CHAPTER
Four

LUNCH WAS SERVED in the garden room, and Susan watched Laelia place wooden bowls of chicken salad on the frosted-glass table. The chairs were white wicker with bright green cushions. The floor beneath them was terrazzo, and like the living room, tropical plants and flowers filled every empty space. "Is the whole house one continuous mixture of elegance and foliage?" she asked.

"Yes," Helen replied graciously. "Of course most of the credit belongs to Kaleb, but I can claim some for the plants. They are my love and my hobby." A twinkle lit up her eyes. "I can tell by your face you've found the island to your liking, too, my dear. Look at the pretty pink flush to her cheeks, Essie Mae. The tropical sun agrees with her."

Essie nodded, but her eyes were on Kaleb. "Perhaps there's another reason for the flush on her pretty cheeks. Maybe Kaleb is flushed as well, though it's difficult to tell since his face resembles Wolf Man's." She clucked her tongue. "You're not in your Arizona silver mine, dear nephew. You're on your magical island where beauty abounds. Why do you insist on assaulting it instead of complementing it? Besides a shave would give Susan a look at your handsome face."

"You're talking to a brick wall, Essie Mae," Helen interjected. "You know how he is. Don't waste your breath."

"Yes, I know how he is," came Essie's caustic reply. "He's as stubborn as his mother."

"We promised we wouldn't discuss our differences in front of the others," Helen reminded her with a scowl.

The two women glowered at one another, and a smile twisted at the corners of Kaleb's mouth. "Forgive them, Susan. They argue and accuse and overlook the truth. Mother is happy on the island and Aunt Essie is happy Stateside. You'll learn to ignore them with time. Despite all their bickering, they're close. It's become a way of life for them."

"Hrump!" Essie muttered, reaching for a honey biscuit. "Just as Kaleb's beachcomber antics have become a way of life for him. Van Gogh would be shamed!"

"It was Gauguin, not van Gogh, who lived in Tahiti," Kaleb teased. "This is Samoa, and if you'll notice, I have both my ears."

Throughout the meal, the banter and put downs continued, but Susan wasn't offended. She knew that sincere affection lay beneath it all. What saddened her was knowing she was the outsider.

When everyone rose from the table to have tea on the veranda, Susan's melancholy was intensified by her awareness of Kaleb's probing eyes. During dessert the reason for her sadness had come clear to her. Her growing love for the island was matched by a growing interest in its master. She would never forget the feel of Kaleb's strong arms, the taste of his mouth, and his words, "A beautiful woman's kiss." But that was all it had meant to him, the pleasure of the moment. He, too, had experienced the deep, heart-felt wounds of a broken romance, but, unlike her, he had determined that no one would ever capture his heart again. Yet now, as she met the cool appraisal in his eyes, she knew it would take very little to conquer her own heart. She must take care. She was open and vulnerable and incapable of surviving another round of heartbreak.

After they had enjoyed cups of spicy orange pekoe tea, Helen described a typical afternoon on the island. "Unfortunately, it's nap time for those of us over fifty. Laelia tends to certain chores and then prepares for the evening meal, while Sam goes to the village to collect eggs and visit his father. So I'm afraid you'll be on your own for several hours. Of course you can call on Kaleb for a bit of company, but dragging him out of his study might prove to be a problem."

Susan's eyes shifted toward Kaleb, but he was deep in thought, his eyes riveted on the dense jungle beyond. If he'd heard his mother's words, he made no response.

"I don't mind having a few hours to myself," Susan assured her, managing a smile. "It will give me time to do some exploring on my own and perhaps even dabble in my paints."

Satisfied, Helen nodded. "Well, then, I suppose we'd best call it an afternoon. Dinner will be served on the veranda at six."

Kaleb looked at her then, and his green eyes glittered. "Explore to your heart's content, my teinetiti, but I wouldn't go too far from the paths you're already familiar with. Our island may look innocent, but it can be dangerous for those who are unaware or stupidly bold. You could find yourself treed by a wild boar or hanging upside down with your foot in a snare. The jungle is full of both."

"Now, now," Helen interrupted, scowling at her son. "There's no point in frightening her."

"I'm not trying to frighten her," Kaleb replied, "but you said yourself she's adventuresome, and I haven't got time to go chasing after her if she chooses to be foolish."

"I won't be foolish, Mr. Knight," Susan bristled, pulling herself up straight and tightening her jaw. "No one need worry. I'm perfectly capable of taking care of myself!" She instantly regretted her words: it was an unfortunate way to end a delightful luncheon, but she thoroughly resented the fact that Kaleb looked upon her as an adventuresome young girl who had to be tied to a tree to be kept out of trouble. What disturbed her even more was the amusement flickering in his eyes.

Still feeling tugs of irritation, Susan stood at the edge of the lagoon in a brief azure-blue bikini and looked up at the towering palms and the backdrop of brilliant blue sky. She was acutely aware of what drew men to the tropics and why some of them stayed. The jungle did more than seduce the heart and emotions. It became part of every breath.

Fastening her hair on top of her head, Susan plunged into the water. With strong, swift strokes, she swam to the middle of the lagoon, where she rolled over and lazily surrendered to the warm, gentle caress of the crystal-clear water. The irritation she hadn't been able to shake since lunch finally melted away. She was glad she had chosen to go swimming. There would be enough time later for prowling about and dipping into her paints. Today, her first day in paradise, she wanted to savor every incredible sensation.

She was stretched out on a towel when Laelia's voice broke through her drifting, sleepy thoughts. "You'll get burned if you're not careful, Miss Susan. Our sun shows no mercy on those who have white skin."

Susan sat up and smiled. "Thank you for your concern, Laelia, but I'm wearing a protective lotion. As a rule, I tan quite easily. What's in the basket?"

Laelia knelt down in the sand and placed the basket in front of Susan. "Mr. Kaleb instructed me to gather up some flowers for your enjoyment." She pointed out Hibiscus, orchids, Blue ginger, Plumeria, and Gardenia, their fragrance reaching up in heady sweetness.

Touched by Kaleb's thoughtfulness, Susan felt a sudden rush of emotion. "It was nice of him to think of me," she said huskily, wondering if it was his way of asking her to forgive him. If so, he had succeeded.

"I shall put them in water for you and then I must return to the big house. I have dinner to prepare." Her brown eyes lowered. "It's almost four o'clock, Miss Susan."

It was Laelia's way of telling her to shake a leg, and Susan smiled. "I'll be ready before six, Laelia, don't worry."

The girl nodded and padded off toward the tree house. Susan grabbed up the towel and caught up with her at the bottom of the stairs. "Laelia, Mr. Knight has called me his teinetiti on several occasions. Could you tell me what it means?"

Laelia faced Susan, but lowered her eyes once again. With her dark skin it was difficult to detect, but Susan was certain she could see a deep flush sweep the girl's cheeks.

"It—It means little girl, Miss Susan."

Long after Laelia had placed the flowers in water and gone back to the main house, Susan fumed, her anger rolling from simmer to boil. His little girl be damned! She was well aware of what Kaleb Knight thought of her.

Was there no end to the ups and downs she must endure because of him? Realizing she was overreacting, she wearily ran bath water and submerged under a frosting of bubbles. She had already warned her injured heart to take care, yet here she was allowing her emotions to run rampant without rhyme or reason. She had to stop this!

Wrapped in a towel, Susan sat on the edge of the bed and considered what to wear. Her first thought was to wear something chic and sexy to make Kaleb look twice before he thought of her as a child or tried to call her his teinetiti. But she hadn't brought along anything chic, let alone sexy, and what did it matter anyway? Dressed in a flour sack or a designer dress, he would still think of her as Essie's little friend, the adventuresome girl who was just a pain in the neck.

Settling on a soft mauve-colored puletasi, she winced when the material touched her skin. One quick look in the floor-length mirror confirmed what Laelia had feared. She had gotten too much sun. Her skin was hot pink. Just her luck! She should have realized that the Samoan sun was stronger than the sun in San Francisco. Damn! Applying a light coating of makeup was pure torture, and when she scrunched up her nose or tried to raise an eyebrow, her whole face contorted into a stiff mask of misery. Her cheeks were the color of a tomato and her nose matched, she thought dejectedly. Here was one more thing to amuse Kaleb Knight.

By the time she had decided what sandals to wear, dabbed Cinnabar behind each ear, and headed for the house, her back and chest were on fire, too. Smiling wouldn't be easy, but smile she must. She would drop dead before revealing her misery to Kaleb—or admitting that she had been foolish. She'd tucked a pale lavender orchid behind her ear, hoping it would offset the rosy glow of her skin, but when she joined the festivities on the veranda, she knew her efforts had been wasted.

"Oh, my!" Essie cried out in dismay. "Oh, my, just look at you!"

"Oh, my!" Helen mirrored, shaking her head. "We should have warned you about the sun."

Kaleb—a transformed Kaleb Knight—stood against the railing, and made no comment, although one dimple flashed and one brow rose. This man, who wore trim tan slacks and a brown silk shirt, was clean-shaven and devastatingly handsome. His hair had been cut, waving over his ears, and if it wasn't for the familiar dimples and jade-green eyes, she wouldn't have recognized him. Trying to regain her composure, she found that the new Kaleb Knight was even more unnerving than his wild and barbaric predecessor.

"Vinegar and water," Essie was saying. "Best we get her into a tub of vinegar and water as soon as possible!"

"No, Essie Mae. I have a medicated spray that will do the trick," Helen announced firmly.

Finding her voice from the depths of her quavering stomach, Susan shook her head. "I'll be all right, really. You're making too much of this. I burn easily and tan quickly. By tomorrow, I'll be golden brown."

"For your sake, I hope you're right," Kaleb spoke up finally. "We're going on a tour of the island, remember?"

How could she forget! She looked up at him, her eyes deepening to purple. "I'm looking forward to it."

"As you might look forward to Armageddon, I would suspect, judging by the expression on your face," Kaleb said, giving her a lazy, amused grin. His lashes lowered, veiling the emerald gleam of his eyes. "Well, you needn't worry. I won't take you into the jungle wilds and seduce you, if that's what you're concerned about."

"Ah, well, I think perhaps we should have Laelia serve cocktails," Helen spoke up quickly, exchanging almost frantic glances with Essie. "Essie and I drink white wine, but perhaps you might enjoy one of Kaleb's concoctions of rum and pineapple juice."

Susan had turned her back on Kaleb, but she heard him move close—close enough to feel his warm breath on her shoulder. "I suggest you try the passion fizz," he whispered in her ear. "It will numb the pain. Your back looks particularly hard hit. It's a very pretty back, I might add."

"I'll have a glass of white wine," Susan said, lifting her chin defiantly, desperately trying to ignore Kaleb's comment. His male scent wafted around her on the soft whisper of a breeze.

Laelia appeared almost instantly with glasses on a tray, and Susan sighed, grateful for a chance to escape her tumultuous thoughts. But as the girl's brown eyes traveled over Susan's sun-scorched skin, she flushed in misery. She alone was responsible for spoiling her first night on Sapphire Island.

Taking her glass, Susan walked over to the railing, as though to rid herself of everything but the night sounds of the jungle coming to life around her. She lifted her face to the soft breeze and watched in awe as the setting sun turned the sky pale gold. Strands of crimson silk sifted across the horizon, mingling and then spreading like a scarlet cloak.

"It's beautiful, don't you think?" Kaleb asked, joining her. She took a sip of wine and nodded. "Something you might want to capture on canvas?" She nodded again, near tears but not knowing why.

"I feel there's a rift of some sort between us," Kaleb said then, grasping her chin gently and tilting it until she had no choice but to meet his smoky green gaze. "I thought we were friends, my teinetiti. Earlier today we shared our lives and much more. Have I done something to upset you? Have I said something to offend you?"

His clear eyes reflected sincere concern, and the tears threatening to fall welled and spilled. "If you want to be my friend, stop calling me your teinetiti,"

she retorted feverishly. "I am *not* your little girl! Nor
am I the innocent child, the adventuresome, silly little
girl you seem to think I am. With every breath you
seem to delight in putting me down, and I thoroughly
dislike you for it!"

A dimple creased his cheek. "Ah, so it comes out.
I suppose you asked Laelia for the meaning of the
word teinetiti? Did she also tell you it's a form of
endearment? Did she tell you the young women of
Samoa cherish the word and hold it as a great compliment?"

Kaleb's eyes remained clear and honest, and Susan
felt strangled with embarrassment. Her face flamed
as she shook her head.

"I thought not. Well, be assured, I meant it as a
compliment. To me, you seem very young and very
innocent. And you're obviously unaware of the
strength of your charms. As for putting you down,
the sun has confused your thoughts. I meant no harm.
I'm a notorious tease, but I only tease those I care
about. If it offends you . . ." His green eyes flashed.
"Why do you suppose I shaved off my beard and
trimmed my hair? It was for you, dear girl. I'm sorry
if I've caused your unhappiness and long face. You're
like a breath of spring and I would be disappointed
if you ended our friendship."

Was he teasing again? Susan couldn't tell, but one
thing was certain. To share Kaleb's life for even a
few moments was an experience never to be forgotten.

"Truce?" he asked softly.

For once, Susan was at a loss for words.

"Ah-hmmmm," Helen called from across the veranda. "Laelia is ready to serve."

"Well?" Kaleb insisted. "Do we enjoy the delights

of Laelia's fine cooking as friends or foe?"

She looked at him warily, her lashes fluttering. "Friends," she said finally, though in her heart she couldn't help but wonder if friendship of any sort was possible with a man like Kaleb Knight.

The table was set with fine china, silver, sweet-smelling flowers, and flickering candles. Susan was seated across from Kaleb, much to her dismay, for no matter where she chose to look, his green eyes met hers in friendly fire. Laelia proved worthy of the praise given. The chicken in a rich cream sauce was heavenly, the rice fluffy and served with bits of onions and tiny water chestnuts. For dessert, pineapple sherbet was scooped up into dainty cut-glass dishes, and the coffee was rich and flavorful. But Susan wasn't hungry. She barely nibbled at the food on her plate, and excused herself right after the coffee had been poured.

"Too much sun," Essie nodded knowingly.

"Too much sun," Helen repeated with concern. "Best get yourself into bed as soon as possible, dear, and if you're not up to the scenic tour tomorrow, just say so."

"I'll see her safely to the tree house," Kaleb intervened. "It's the least I can do to make amends for our treacherous sun. What Susan needs is a cool bath followed by cold compresses. Later, a pure cold cream can be rubbed on her skin to add moisture. With luck, she'll be as good as new in a few days. But if she's not up to bumping around the island tomorrow, she should say so." He was looking down at her now, and his eyes reflected as much concern as his voice. "Did you hear what I said, Susan?"

She heard, and was filled with frustration. She did

not want to be doted upon, especially by Kaleb Knight, but it would seem she had little choice. When she took a few steps, nausea swept over her, and she felt light-headed. In despair and with a weak nod, she succumbed to the strength and protection of his arms.

By the light from strategically placed floodlights and with a firm grip on Susan's arm, Kaleb led the way to the lagoon. When they'd reached the steps to the tree house, he lifted her into his arms without ceremony and maneuvered the steps with ease.

Too sick to protest, Susan allowed him to run a tub of water and even hold the towel while she shed her clothing. But once she was submerged in the cool, clear water and Kaleb made no move toward the door, she became incensed. "Get out!" she screamed, swishing the water into a tidal wave across the bathroom floor. "Damn you, Kaleb Knight!"

His deep rolling laughter filled the room. "I see you're not *too* sick." He stretched his arms, rippling muscles beneath his shirt, while his eyes flickered over her drawn up legs and arms clasped across her chest. "You're a rarity in our modern world, and that's not a put down. You're like my birds. You soar with grace and beauty and then squawk when restrained. But I won't restrain you now." A dimple flashed. "By the way, the flush to your skin is most appealing. Sleep well, my teinetiti."

Susan's heart pounded as she sought words of retaliation, but it was too late. By the time she untangled her tongue, Kaleb had gone, striding away without a backward glance.

CHAPTER
Five

DARKNESS WAS GRADUALLY lifting toward the east when Susan stirred the next morning. She stretched, gingerly testing the tautness of her skin and, finding it only a little tender, decided she would survive after all. She'd slept well considering the unnerving events of the previous evening.

After lying awake for some time fretting over her feelings, wondering what she actually felt for the man who had somehow managed to claim a portion of her heart, she had finally come to grips with the situation. There was no doubt Kaleb Knight was a complex man, and it would probably take a lifetime to truly understand him, but that didn't really matter. She had only three weeks to enjoy Sapphire Island, and she

48

would be foolish indeed if she allowed the maddening man who reigned supreme to disrupt her good fortune.

Now, however, sitting on the edge of the bed, listening to the chorus of twittering birds in the nearby jungle, she also knew that if her heart became entangled, her determination to avoid involvement would disappear on the whisper of the wind.

But her main concern right now was how to sit astride a horse fully clothed when her pink-tinged body still ached.

Slipping into a soft flowered robe, Susan headed for the kitchen, hoping to find some coffee. A freshly perked pot awaited her on the stove—and Kaleb sat sprawled in a kitchen chair, cup in hand. Good god, had he spent the night? Had her dreams of sensuous lips, jade-green eyes and passionate embraces been real?

His gaze lingered over her flushed face and tumbled hair. "Did you sleep well?" he asked.

"Good morning," she returned coolly. "Yes, I slept well. Would you mind telling me what you're doing here?"

"I wanted to share your first Samoan sunrise," he drawled, flashing dimples and his superlative white teeth.

Her velvet eyes traveled the length of him, taking in the trim, tight-fitting jeans, gauzy Navaho shirt, turquoise belt, and polished riding boots. She could not stop her appraising gaze. Flustered, but satisfied he hadn't stayed the night after all, that her dreams had only been dreams, she managed a smile. "You look as though you're ready to spend the day on horseback." She moved to the stove and poured coffee into a mug he'd set out. "Unfortunately, I won't be as well attired. Faded blue jeans, shirt, and sneakers will be the best I can do."

"Do you feel up to this?" he queried.

"Of course." She sat down at the table across from him.

"Well, then, I don't suppose the horse will mind what you're wearing." He grinned crookedly. "The sun is up. Let's take our coffee outside."

She followed him onto the veranda, where she gasped with delight. The world around them was enveloped in a soft golden blanket as the sun's rays climbed over the palms. The lagoon shimmered like a jewel in a jungle setting.

"This is why I chose this spot for the tree house," Kaleb said quietly. "I wanted to be able to stand as I'm doing now and feel the warmth of each new day."

She couldn't see his face, but she could sense his sadness. Her heart pounded in response.

He whistled softly and the birds came, soaring across the lagoon and landing on a tree branch near the veranda. "Do they follow you everywhere?" Susan asked, delighted to see them again.

"They're never far away."

The bird called Tasi swooped, landing on Susan's shoulder. "Do you suppose she remembers me?"

"It would appear so. You could probably tame her as your own with a little work and patience. She's obviously chosen you as a special friend." His eyes, as green as the deep sea, slipped over her face as though searching for some glimmer of interest.

A great lump constricted Susan's throat. She would like nothing better than to befriend the beautiful bird and tame it as her own, but doing so would add to the growing list of reasons why, when the time came, it was going to be difficult to say good-bye. "I have less than three weeks," she said finally, unable to meet Kaleb's eyes. "I'm afraid getting too close to Tasi would make leaving the island even more difficult."

"But you can always return," he reasoned. "There will be another trip another day."

"I doubt it. I couldn't possibly afford a trip like this on my own, and I certainly couldn't expect Essie to foot the bill again. I only agreed to come along this time because she insisted, knowing how desperately I needed to get away and because she thought I might help convince your mother to move Stateside."

Kaleb shook his head. "Aunt Essie has been trying to talk Mother into moving to San Francisco for years, but she's fighting a losing battle. Perhaps she just wanted the company."

"Perhaps."

Removing the bird from Susan's shoulder, Kaleb studied her for a long moment, then reached out to touch her cheek, moving his fingers down, tracing the line of her chin.

At his touch, she swayed, meeting his eyes with her own, open and vulnerable. If he were to take her in his arms . . .

But Kaleb pulled his hand away as though stung and backed up, his face a hard mask. "Get dressed," he said abruptly. "Laelia will have breakfast waiting, and Sam will fetch the horses. The day will be a long and trying one unless we get an early start."

She gazed up at him, at the tyrant who assumed the arrogance of a king one moment and acted gentle and caring the next. He was a complex man, a mixture of feelings and contradictions she doubted she could ever sort out. With a deep sigh of regret, she headed for the bedroom.

Within an hour, they were riding along the beach mounted on two magnificent Arabians who traversed the white sand with ease. Kaleb had explained while they were having breakfast how they would follow the beach until they reached the narrow river that spilled into the blue Pacific. Then, turning inland, they would follow paths along the river until they reached the village.

Susan was baffled by Kaleb's moodiness. He had wanted to share the sunrise with her, and for a time, while they were captured in the middle of the golden cage of early morning, he had acted like a friend. But now she found herself traveling with a stranger whose lips were pulled tight and whose eyes remained veiled.

Off to a rather wretched start herself, she had wanted to weep when she'd tried pulling on tight-fitting blue jeans. Her skin was much too tender to tolerate restriction of any sort, so she had had to settle on the lightweight baggy pants and shirt she used for painting. Kaleb had presented her with a floppy, do-pey-looking straw hat to protect her pink cheeks and rosy nose. She hadn't argued. What would be the point? In his present mood, the day did not bode well in any case.

They turned inland at the river. Susan was bursting with appreciation, but the expression on Kaleb's face kept her silent. Still, there was no way she could contain the inner joy she felt. The river, though wide in spots, was dark with overhanging foliage and dripping flowers. She spotted a variety of orchids, but most of the blooms were exotic and unknown to her.

They rode through tunnels of vines, forests of coconut palms, and jungle trees with moss-covered branches. Everywhere the branches were alive with hooting, twittering, skittering creatures.

At one point, they came to a clearing where the sun's rays, sifting through the trees like a dusting of gold, dazzled Susan's senses. As the sun danced off the man and horse in front of her, she couldn't help but notice that Kaleb's hair was the same color as the stallion. They looked as though they were welded together as one. How proudly he sat in the saddle.

"We're almost there," Kaleb announced finally, striking out again through a patch of taro.

Susan sighed with relief. She was eager to see the village and meet its people, anxious to be distracted from her glum companion.

Within moments, the terrain changed. They had entered a small but verdant valley bounded on three sides by towering palms and stately old teaks. To the south lay the blue Pacific. The village formed the center, and tiny naked children ran to greet them as they entered the compound of thatched huts. A black dog barked at the heels of Susan's dappled mare until Kaleb's voice commanded, "Off with you!" The dog slunk away with its tail between its legs, and Susan could sympathize with the way it felt. She, too, had felt the force of Kaleb's displeasure.

Brown-skinned women wearing puletasis of every description waved, and then continued about their business. From a hut larger than the others, set off to one side, stepped a giant man.

"Chief Fua," Kaleb told Susan, dismounting and helping her to do the same. "He has the highest title in the village."

"Is that why his hut is larger than the others?" she queried.

"Yes, but it's not a hut. It's called a fale. He shares his fale with his family. His brother, Nea, is Sam's father. He's also a matai, the head of his household. Here many relatives live together and divide the tasks of work, housekeeping, and cooking."

As they approached the chief, women and children came out of several fales, soon joined by the few men who were about. Smoke from a stone pit filled the air, along with the aroma of cooking food. The women smiled shyly, and the men shook hands with Kaleb, although their eyes lingered on Susan.

"Talofa," Chief Fua grinned, extending his hand with great ceremony. His well-muscled body shone in the morning sunlight. He was probably well over seventy but looked half that old. He wore a red waist-to-the-ground wraparound skirt, and his bare feet, though covered with dust, looked toughened enough to tread over hot coals.

Kaleb gripped the old man's hand. "Talofa, Chief Fua. I've brought a friend. This is Susan McRay."

The old man's warm brown eyes danced as he took Susan's hand. "Talofa, Miss Susan. You are even prettier than Samala described."

"Sam," Kaleb explained, sensing Susan's puzzlement. "My father shortened it to Sam."

A girl appeared then, followed by a tall, handsome man, and Susan stood enraptured while introductions were made. The girl was Laelia's sister, and the man was her husband. Their names were Luina and Tuai and they made a spectacular looking couple. Luina was obviously pregnant, but it was her lovely face that had quickened Susan's artistic senses. She had high cheekbones, expressive almond eyes, and a straight nose. Reluctant to ask if she might do a sketch of the girl at some later time, and fearful of appearing foolish, Susan tucked the idea away for safekeeping until she had an opportunity to discuss it with Laelia.

In the fale they sat on woven mats and were served hot tea in coconut shell cups. The chief chuckled when Susan expressed surprise at the taste. "It is unlike the tea you are accustomed to, Miss Susan. It is made from withered leaves of wild orange. Not unlike what I believe you call orange pekoe."

It was wonderfully delicious, and while she took tiny sips, savoring its flavor, she listened to the conversation going on around her. The chief aired the village problems while Kaleb listened attentively, offering suggestions where he could. Then the talk turned to fishing and the weather. Finally, sensing that Susan might become restless listening to "man talk," the chief called on Luina to show her around the village. Kaleb warned her not to wander off as it was near noon and they wouldn't be staying long.

Susan followed Luina out into the sun-splashed compound. "Mr. Kaleb is like one of us," Luina smiled, leading Susan toward the cooking pit. "We all miss him when he leaves the island." She looked at Susan through long, sweeping lashes. "You like Mr. Kaleb?"

There was little doubt as to what the girl was implying. There was also little point in trying to hide her feelings. The Samoans were very perceptive. "Yes, I like Mr. Kaleb," Susan said, flushing under her sunburned cheeks.

Luina laughed and took Susan's hand. "If you marry him, you can also be one of us, Miss Susan.

We could become good friends. Like family."

They had reached the cooking pit, and Susan quickly turned away, not wanting to meet the girl's eyes. Marry Kaleb? How could she possibly respond to that?

"In the oven, bananas, yams, breadfruit, taro, shell fish, fish, and chicken will cook until done," Luina explained. "This is cooking day. Enough food must be prepared to feed the village for two days. On the next cooking day, someone else will tend the oven."

The old woman who sat near the pit—or the oven, as Luina called it—smiled as they walked by. No matter where Susan looked, she sensed happiness and contentment. Everyone had a task, but the mood was relaxed, slow-paced, and happy.

For the next half hour or so, Susan watched old women weave baskets and old men repair the fales, replacing palm leaves where needed. She took special delight in a group of nursing mothers who had congregated under a shady tree. Modesty was an unfamiliar notion among them, and Susan found their naturalness delightfully refreshing.

"Most of the men," Luina explained, "are out gathering coconuts or fishing off the reef. The able women who are without children are in the fields weeding or gathering food for the next cooking day. Some of the children collect water, and some try to help in the fields. Soon the sun will be high and it will be time to eat. After that will follow several hours of sleep. When it is cool again, we will have our evening meal. Nights are the most fun. Sometimes the whole village will go to the water and fish by torchlight. Sometimes we will dance until very late, until the moon has set in the sky. Sometimes lovers will walk to the beach."

Feeling overwhelmed and euphoric at Luina's descriptive tales of how they all worked, played, and loved, Susan could find no words to speak.

They stopped last at the fale belonging to Luina and Laelia's family. Nuta, their mother, welcomed Susan with a hug and a cool drink of spring water. She was the sister of Mutu, the uncle who had crafted the lovely bed and kitchen table in the tree house. Nuta was a plump, bright-eyed little woman, and it was she who led the way to the small fale where Mutu carved his wood. Mutu was an adorable little man with snow-white hair and large brown eyes. Susan would have been content to watch him work for the remainder of the day, but Kaleb appeared then, and it was time to go.

They walked to where the horses were tethered to a tree, exchanging waves and hugs with everyone. It was difficult to say good-bye, and a long time passed before Susan could trust her voice to speak. Soon she grew hungry and tired. Even in baggy clothing and a floppy hat, her sunburn was a misery to endure.

"How much further?" she asked of a silent, seemingly preoccupied Kaleb.

"We're almost there."

His words barely spoken, they began to climb, gradually at first, then more steeply over masses of tangled vines. Susan thought they'd lost the trail among the mossy rocks and thick, feathery ferns, but then just as quickly as the ascent had begun, they reached the summit, the top of the island, the top of the world. Below, the surf thundered against cavernous rocks, and beyond, the Pacific stretched out into infinity, it's turquoise water melting into sapphire and then to shades of blue-gray on the horizon.

Susan felt her stomach curl at the frothy sight below. She wasn't usually fearful of heights, but the cliff was narrow—no more than two feet across in spots—and a wave of dizziness almost overtook her.

Kaleb turned, surveying her with one quizzically raised brow. "Think you can make it down to the beach?"

"A-Aren't we going to have a picnic on the cliffs?" she asked hesitantly.

"It's a bit too breezy, and you're looking rather pale under your rosy glow. We'd better head down before you faint away. We can explore the cliffs another day."

The breeze rippled Susan's hat, but it wasn't gale force by any means. He was leading her down the narrow trail because he felt she couldn't handle the staggering heights and the sight of the ominous rocks below. He was treating her like a child again, and she was powerless to stop him.

"I could've managed the cliffs," Susan bristled as soon as they'd reached the beach and dismounted. She crooked her neck to look back. Had they really been that far up?

"Sure, and you might have gotten vertigo and fallen over the edge, too. As I said, we'll save it for another day. Meanwhile, enjoy the view from the bottom. This is called Ke Beach, the beach of no return."

It was Susan's turn to lift a brow. "Meaning?"

"Meaning at high tide there's no way out. Come on, let's see what Laelia packed for lunch, or the day will be gone and the food wasted on the gulls."

The little beach was indeed walled in. Surf and rock lay behind them now, though she could still hear the deafening crescendo. Further on, an outcropping of rocks and foliage graced the base of a magnificent waterfall. Kaleb led the horses here and tethered them to a tree beside a fresh-water pool.

From the saddlebags, he extracted a small knapsack that had been carefully packed with generous portions of fried chicken, cheese, crackers, honey biscuits, and fruit. The bottle of red wine was the surprise, and Laelia had even thought to include plastic glasses.

"You look done in," Kaleb said, handing her a glass of wine. "And a bit preoccupied, too, I might add. Penny for your thoughts."

Susan sipped the wine and managed a smile. "If you must know, I was thinking how difficult you are to understand. One minute you act as though you want to be friends and the next minute I could swear you hate me." She couldn't meet his eyes, feeling incredibly vulnerable and unsure of what his response might be.

"Don't worry," Kaleb countered harshly. "If you understood the true Kaleb Knight, you might pack up and fly out tonight. Cheers."

They touched glasses. Susan supposed she should be angered by his attitude, but there was something in his voice—was it a touch of regret? It carried a protective ring she didn't understand. "Oh, I think I could handle the true Kaleb Knight if he'd give me half a chance," she said lightly, though she had to struggle for her next breath.

His eyes flashed to her face. "Is that so? Perhaps we should put that to the test one day soon."

She knew what he meant, and panic tumbled through her. She was already attracted to him, and was sure to fail any test, emotional or physical, he set up for her.

He gave a brief, hard laugh. "Don't look so worried, my teinetiti. I don't go around attacking beautiful young women without provocation."

Was he teasing again? She couldn't tell as the sweep of his lashes veiled his eyes. He had kissed her not twenty-four hours before. Had he forgotten? Or did he actually see her as a child, a bothersome girl who had to be kept at arm's length. She glanced down at her paint-splattered clothing, dusty socks, and well-worn sneakers. What could she expect dressed in such absurd attire? Besides, every time she was near the man and looked into his deep green eyes, she felt foolish and immature.

He handed her a chicken leg. "Eat heartily, love. We still have half the island to cover."

"I've enjoyed every moment so far," she told him truthfully. "Especially the village and its people. I'd love to do a sketch of Luina and maybe Mutu while he's at work. Do you think they'd mind?"

"I'm sure they'd be flattered." He slanted her a disconcerting glance. "Just don't try and reach the village by yourself, hear?"

"I promise." She wiped her hands on a paper napkin and then stretched back in the shade of a fringe-tipped palm.

"But do you mean it?" Kaleb pressed. "I already know you're adventuresome, and strong-willed. It's not so much the thought of seeing you lost that bothers me, but the picture of you up a tree in a snare or facing a red-eyed, snorting boar. I told you before, there are plenty of both." He stopped, waiting for her reaction, but she just gazed past him toward the glorious blue Pacific.

"Perhaps if I tell you about what happened to me

when I was ten years old, you might understand the importance of what I'm trying to tell you."

This time Susan's violet eyes searched his face, peering at him from under the brim of her hat. He seemed sincerely concerned, and for some reason she felt flattered. "I understand the importance of what you're saying, Kaleb, honestly I do, but I'd like to hear the story anyway."

He was looking at her in a way that made her pulse race. His russet head of tousled hair glinted in the sun, his eyes lightened a shade of green, and his dimples creased—he was so handsome!

A slight grimness touched his mouth. "Even at ten years old I knew every inch of the island. But I also knew how stupid it was to get off the beaten path. The heart of the jungle is no place for anyone but the natives who search for stray chickens, wild bananas, and avocados, or hunt a piglet for their fia fia—that's their Samoan feast. Our island may be small compared to others, but the interior is as wild as it was centuries ago.

"Anyway, as an adventuresome, headstrong child myself, and because I'd had an argument with my father, I struck out toward the village, cross-country so to speak. They found me a day later, hanging upside down in a tree. I'd been caught up in the snare meant for a boar who taunted me through the whole ordeal. He had come at dusk, snorting and charging the spot just below where my head hung. A few inches further down and he would've had me. I was unconscious when they found me—a blessed escape from my nightmare of fear. Though the island is very beautiful and gentle, it can be utterly treacherous."

His story brought a chill to Susan. "How frightening," she whispered, visualizing the horrors he must have endured because of his careless judgment.

Kaleb merely grinned. "Don't get upset. I didn't mean to ruin your day, just warn you." He studied her intently, his eyes green flames of amusement. "I suppose I can imagine you being youthfully indiscreet, love, and it's my job to protect everyone on my island."

It wasn't what he said but his manner that inflamed Susan. The man's bold arrogance was maddening! "Submitting to a youthful indiscretion now and again is what keeps a person young," she flung back at him, "and that's certainly better than being stuffy."

"Are you calling me stuffy?" he asked, a curious light in his eyes.

"If the shoe fits . . . I get the impression you don't understand me, and that's what makes you so wretched."

"Stuffy and wretched. Is there anything else you'd care to add to the list?"

"Yes, you're hateful," she choked. "One minute you're trying to protect me from the evils of your island and the next you're putting me down as a youthful idiot. I'm tired of listening to you mock my feelings every time I turn around. Do you make a practice of collecting scalps from every ordinary female you meet?"

"There's nothing ordinary about you," he assured her tightly. "And I'm sorry if I upset you. Are you ready to go on? Or do you want to rest a little longer?"

Susan wanted nothing more than to climb on her horse and ride away, simply outrace this devil. But her anger consumed all reason, stopping her from even making the attempt. "I think I'd like to drink another glass of wine and rest a little longer," she said, lifting her chin defiantly.

Without responding, Kaleb filled her glass and set about packing up what was left of their picnic lunch. That done, he stripped off his shirt and jeans and, wearing crisp blue bathing trunks, headed for the surf. Susan watched as he dove through the waves with the ease of a dolphin. She took off her hat, and using it as a pillow, lay back and closed her eyes. The soft breeze ruffled her hair; the sand felt warm and comforting. She listened to the cry of a gull and its answering mate, to the surf as it swept ashore. She had never known such sweet contentment. Despite her many anxieties and unsettled feelings, she felt her muscles relax as she was swept away in slumber.

The whinny of a horse awakened her with a start. Disoriented at first, and then realizing she was still on the beach, her eyes fluttered open and a flush swept across her cheeks. Kaleb was sitting beside her, quietly watching her through unreadable eyes. She struggled to sit up, grappling with her emotions. Beads of water still clung to him, and the sun's rays danced off the droplets in his hair. Staring at him, she seemed to be drowning in each little rivulet, unable to escape the pull of her own desire.

He gazed down at her for what seemed an eternity—until she could scarcely breathe, until the breeze of sea and sky had become a violent wind. When his mouth covered hers, trapping her cry of protest, she surrendered, clinging to his damp body with a fever she wasn't aware she possessed. His kiss was unbearably sweet and gentle, causing her stomach to contract and her back to arch, meeting the hardness of him. His scent filled her senses as her mouth moved under his, accepting the warmth of his breath that was suddenly her own. Did she love this man whose gentle touch contained the powers of heaven and hell? Could she love him? Or had desire overshadowed reason?

Kaleb's mouth slid to the softness of her throat, and with a groan, he sat up. "I must be out of my mind," he said sharply, though his hands were shaking.

Susan's warm body felt as rejected as yesterday's news, and tears welled near the surface. "I'm sorry you find kissing me such a bore," she muttered, choking over the pain in her heart. Damn Kaleb Knight and everything he stood for! And damn her heart for wanting his love!

Displaying the arrogant self-control she was learning to hate, Kaleb stood up and slipped into his clothing. A smile tugged at the corners of his mouth though his eyes were cold. "You know your feelings and I know mine, my teinetiti. I told you I don't go around attacking beautiful young women. There's no way you can understand how I feel."

"Just as there's no way you can understand how I feel, you—you brute!"

Green ice glazed over her amethyst glare. "Ah, but I *do* understand, love, and that's why we're getting the hell out of here. You may have just escaped a stormy engagement, but you're still very desirable. But I refuse to play the villain and take advantage of your broken heart and vulnerability. You'll be going home soon, and someday, when you meet the man of your dreams, you'll look back and thank me for my self-control."

"I hate you!"

"Do you now? Good, then you'll be safe enough."

With her heart pounding, she stood and faced Kaleb squarely. "It's really incredible. No matter what I do or say, you somehow manage to twist things around and make me look like a fool—" She broke off, biting her lip in frustration. "And I can see by the expression on your face that I'm wasting my breath. Well, go ahead and amuse yourself at my expense. And while you're at it, you can go straight to hell!"

Brows arched and dimples flashed. "We'd best be on our way, love. I think perhaps you've had too much sun. Grumpiness doesn't become you."

Nor does arrogance become you, Susan thought dismally as they led the horses to the path at the top of the cliff.

CHAPTER
Six

TO SUSAN'S SURPRISE the ride back was pleasant. Kaleb's change of mood was as swift as a summer storm. He chatted amiably, pointing out various trees and flowers he thought might interest her.

Managing to put aside what had happened at the beach, as well as her confused feelings, Susan began to relax. Her skin was still hot and painful, and her legs ached from sitting astride a horse for so many hours, but she took delight in each new experience, grasping, once again, the magic of the island.

They made a full circle and rode in from the east, through a grove of coconut palms, across a stream, and then into the stable area where Sam was grooming a magnificent gray stallion. Sam looked up and waved.

Susan's quick intake of breath brought a chuckle to Kaleb's lips. "He's a beauty, don't you think?"

"Oh, he's a beauty, all right!" Susan exclaimed, quickly dismounting and hurrying toward the lovely Arabian. "Sam, he's gorgeous!"

Sam flashed a toothy smile and nodded while Susan wrapped her arms around the horse's velvet neck, uttering little sounds for his ears alone.

"Look at that, Sam," Kaleb intoned cheerily. "Have you ever seen Moonflight respond to anyone like that?"

Sam shook his head. "No, Mr. Kaleb. Miss Susan must have a way with horses."

"A far better way with horses than with members of the opposite sex, I would think," Kaleb teased.

"Why didn't you ride this beauty today?" she asked, shooting him a murderous look.

"He's Sam's horse to ride, though I don't know why he bothers. I gave up on the beast a long time ago. He was never broken properly and has a mind of his own. He's rather like a spirited child who knows right from wrong but doesn't give a damn."

It was another dig, and she stiffened. "Perhaps there's a lack of communication between the two of you," she retorted dryly. "It's possible his preferences are as opinionated as your own."

Quite suddenly, Kaleb threw his head back in laughter, though his mouth became firm as he said, "Some men are taken in by a horse's spirit and beauty as well as by a woman's, but I don't happen to be one of them. The island has taught me many things and discretion heads the list. Discretion has kept many a man from hanging by his heart."

"One would have to have a heart before one could

hang from it," Susan replied, her eyes flashing amethyst fire. Too bad if he knew she considered him a devil in paradise.

His smile was indescribably wicked. "And I suppose you consider yourself a judge of men's hearts? Well, you'd better review your homework, my teinetiti. You still have a lot to learn."

Susan bit back the words she wanted to fling at him. No reply of hers would benefit either of them, so giving the horse one final pat, she turned and headed for the house.

Kaleb caught up with her at the pond, but she didn't slow her steps. Every instinct told her to stop and have it out with him, to express her frustrations once and for all, but to do so would undoubtedly bring on the rush of tears swimming close to the surface. And a stupid, childish display at this point was the last thing she needed.

"You'd better put a smile on your sour face, love," came Kaleb's caustic words, "or Mother will assume we've been fighting."

Now she did stop and face him, her anger and frustration complete. "Well, haven't we?" She glared at him through the depths of purple fire. "We've been at odds ever since we met, and I'm tired of playing your crazy games. Pick a daisy and pull the petals. He likes me, he likes me not. Today we're friends, tomorrow we're not. Maybe you can handle that kind of a relationship, but I can't. No wonder your little partner in love tossed you over the cliff. I doubt any woman could learn to live with your arrogance and maddening moods!" She closed her eyes and fought down panic. It had been a dreadful thing to say, and she regretted it the moment the words were spoken.

Quickly, he thrust out his hand and grabbed her hair, tugging her head backwards until her hat fell off and she was forced to meet his icy glare. "What do you know about love," he taunted. "You cry because the love of your life left you for someone else. Have you ever asked yourself why? Perhaps he found the passion of a woman more gratifying than the infatuation of a child."

Susan's head pounded with fury. "You're despicable!" she hissed between clenched teeth. "There is more to love than passion. Love is pure and full of understanding and truth! But, of course, you wouldn't know anything about that."

"And you live in a dream world where puppy dogs talk and marriages are made in heaven, my teinetiti. Love is just a four-letter word like any other. You talk about my arrogance and maddening moods and you're quick to condemn, but you're equally guilty. One minute you act so innocent I'd slay dragons to protect you. The next minute you're a temptress whose violet eyes could melt a man's soul, and I'd give that soul to be able to make love to you."

"And when you're not slaying dragons or wanting to make love to me, you're being hateful," Susan choked, struggling to pull away from him.

But he held her fast, his green eyes glimmering between thick lashes. "Then I suppose I shall have to spend my time slaying dragons or making love to you," he taunted, "though I'd much prefer the latter."

The scent of Gardenia mingled with frangipani floated through the air, filling Susan's head with a dizzy buzz—or was her lightheadedness because of the man who held her close? The man whose eyes burned with desire, turning her legs to rubber as she swayed against him.

"Does it bother you to know I'm aroused by you?" Kaleb whispered huskily, placing gentle kisses across her brow and nose.

Beyond words, her traitorous heart numbing her senses to everything but the feel of her body burning in his arms, Susan reached up, tangling her fingers in his thick hair. She moaned as his mouth traveled along the contours of her neck, coming to rest on the frantic beating of her pulse, that soft, vulnerable spot on her throat. His arms tightened around her as his mouth swept up, covering her own in the ecstasy of a fiery kiss. She could feel the muscles of his thighs, the hardness of his chest, his pounding heart, and the slow, searching pressure enveloping her, consuming her in passionate white fire. He shuddered against her as he murmured her name between kisses. Oh, how she wanted him. How she needed this maddening man who would be king. The warmth and glory of the sun were no match for the sparks igniting between them.

It was Kaleb who finally pulled away. Although his breath was ragged, he was in control, the jade-green of his eyes taking on devilish glints. "You should have been a witch, Susan McRay. Only a witch could cause temporary insanity. Believe me, it won't happen again."

"You're mad!" Susan cried, backing away from him. The breeze was up, ruffling her hair and cooling her inflamed cheeks.

"It's madness mixed up with the wonders of the flesh, and it proves you've barely tasted love."

"Lust, you mean!" Susan flung heatedly.

Kaleb's eyes caressed her, but when he spoke, his voice was void of emotion. "There's little difference between love and lust, my teinetiti, but you won't learn it from me. Run along now, like a good girl, and tell Mother we're back. I'll be there shortly."

Just like that, she was dismissed. With a snap of his fingers, she was supposed to obey. To him, she was nothing more than another tamed bird coming to his call. He took his pleasure, and cast her aside when the game became a bore. He was truly mad, and she would never allow herself to be alone with him again.

It had been an exhausting day, physically as well as mentally, draining Susan to the point of tears. She hadn't gone back to the house, but instead, skirted the velvety lawn and headed for the tree house, where she'd called Helen to give her Kaleb's message. Dinner, Helen had announced, would be at seven o'clock on the veranda, but after Susan hung up, her stomach churned. Food was the last thing on her mind.

Angry with herself because she couldn't seem to stop her silly tears, Susan ran a bath and soaked for an hour. The lobster-look she'd acquired from the Samoan sun was beginning to change to a rich, golden tan. Too bad it wasn't going to be as easy to forget the feel of Kaleb's arms—the taste of his lips, or the passionate lights in his deep green eyes.

Every movement of her body seemed to submerge her further into melancholy. Couldn't she at least be honest with herself? She'd run away from the heartbreak of a broken romance only to be plummeted into another situation, one that was proving to be even more devastating than her entanglement with Paul. Ironically, she wasn't at all certain she even liked the man, and that seemed to be the definitive blow. She had given herself to Paul because she had loved him totally, but to literally throw herself into the arms of a man she barely knew proved that she was as mad as the arrogant man who had claimed her lips and jostled her senses.

The afternoon sun had dipped behind the palms, though it was still warm. Padding into the kitchen dressed in a gauzy wrap, locating instant tea, ice cubes, and a long-handled spoon, she stirred up a glass and drank it down. She felt parched. She felt ravaged! How could she have allowed herself to get so involved? Especially after she'd been so determined to take care. She'd known from their first meeting that she was attracted to the man, yet she'd lost control and walked off the plank. Even now, after sorting it all out and bracing herself with added determination, she could feel her pounding heart as her body responded to Kaleb's touch.

Carrying the second glass of iced tea out onto the veranda, Susan sat down and closed her eyes. It was cooler now. The scent of the island wafted in on a breeze, reminding her of where she was and why. Her time was precious. Too soon, she would be winging her way home, and then it would be too late. She had come to heal her wounds, not open them. The magic of the island was hers to enjoy. She would dress and face the evening anew—and all the days to come.

Susan reached the main house a little before seven, and, joining the festivities on the veranda, was met by Kaleb's flash of dimples and white teeth, one rather shadowy, appreciative glance and then total withdrawal, as though he couldn't be bothered with giving her more than a perfunctory nod.

She had dressed with care, choosing a creamy yellow puletasi that set her newly acquired tan aglow. Adding a white Hibiscus to her upswept hair, she'd felt ready for just about anything, even facing the slayer of dragons. But now she felt miffed, as well as a little breathless. Kaleb wore slim white slacks and a white silk shirt. Several bottons were undone to reveal his muscular, deeply tanned chest, and casting her eyes away from that appealing, vulnerable spot that no doubt smelled of musky cologne, and reminding herself that his aloofness would make her life considerably easier, she turned her attention toward Essie and Helen.

After a round of hugs and compliments, Helen announced she and Essie were leaving for Tutuila in the morning on a shopping spree. "At first, we considered asking you to come along, dear Susan, but then we decided that following our elderly footsteps around for two or three days would be a bore."

"And it's not as though we're leaving you alone," Essie interjected. "We're taking Laelia along, of course, but Sam will be here . . . and Kaleb."

Both women glanced toward Kaleb, but he was standing against the railing with his back to them, apparently lost in thought.

Helen looked perplexed. "Well, for heavens sake! I thought the two of you might have become good friends after spending a whole day together, but from the expression on Susan's face, I'd say the sight of Kaleb's back is more welcome than the setting sun. Kaleb, will you please join our conversation? Did you hear what I said?"

"I heard. You're going to Tutuila for a few days

and want me to play host." He had turned to face them, and his eyes were dark green. "I'm behind schedule on my book now, Mother, and I'm afraid looking after Miss McRay isn't on my agenda. She can always call on Sam if some disaster develops, but I doubt she'll require my full attention."

"I wouldn't dream of imposing on Mr. Knight for any reason," Susan flung heatedly. She managed a smile. "I think it's wonderful that the two of you have the chance to go off together and do some shopping. Where will you stay?"

"With friends," Helen replied, breathing a little easier, though her eyes kept darting from Susan to Kaleb and then to Essie. "Sam radioed the seaplane and the Nelsons. They are old and very dear friends, Susan. Essie hasn't seen them in ages. It should be a pleasant little holiday."

"*If* you don't have to worry about me," Susan added, widening her smile for their benefit. "Well, don't. I'm perfectly able to take care of myself. I've been hoping to paint several canvases, and can't think of a better time to start than tomorrow. The two of you run along and have a good time, you hear?"

Both women looked relieved, and Kaleb turned back to the railing. Laelia padded onto the veranda, and served drinks filled with tinkling ice. Susan deliberately accepted a glass of Kaleb's fiery "passion fizz," shifting her eyes to see if he was watching. He wasn't.

"The only thing I regret, Susan, my dear," Helen said rather quickly, "is that you'll have to fend for yourself as far as meals are concerned. You can use the kitchen here or at the cottage. Either way, there will be plenty of food. Laelia spent the day making casseroles for the men, and I'm sure they won't mind sharing."

"I'd rather concentrate on my painting and stay in the tree house," Susan interrupted. "Just as Mr. Knight seems to be with his writing, I'm a bit of a bore when it comes to painting. I become thoroughly engrossed and would much rather grab a sandwich than prepare a meal. Artist's license," she grinned.

"But you'll be sure and eat, eh?" Essie queried, concern etching her dear face.

Kaleb turned away from the railing. "Like Miss McRay said, she can take care of herself, Aunt Essie."

He seemed perturbed, and their eyes met, deep emerald flames flickering against cool lilac.

"Well, yes, of course, dear," Helen intervened, "but Susan *is* our guest, and what kind of a hostess would I be if I wasn't concerned? As you should be concerned, I might add. Your Arizona desert ways are becoming a habit with you. Your life has become too harsh." She broke off, biting at her lip.

Kaleb shrugged. "Life *is* harsh, Mother. It's the law of the desert."

"But you're not in the desert tonight, my dear nephew," Essie muttered. "You're on Sapphire Island where life is soft and beautiful. Watch your tongue!"

Kaleb merely smiled. "Don't get excited, Aunt Essie. I'm aware of the pleasures on Sapphire Island."

Laelia announced dinner was ready, and again, the women looked relieved at the interruption. Ready or not, Susan couldn't have cared less. The "passion fizz" had given her a buzz, and she hadn't felt so relaxed in weeks.

•   •   •

Dinner was nearing its end, a meal of superb tastes and textures. An excellent crab bisque had been served first, followed by a rack of pork with apple stuffing, and for dessert, fresh coconut pie.

Coffee came next, and then healthy snifters of brandy. Still a little fuzzy from the passion fizz, Susan carried her drink to the railing, breathing in the sounds of the night and the sight of snowflake stars twinkling in the blue-black sky. It was beautiful, refreshingly cool after the heat of the day. She began to hum an old melody that had recently been updated into a contemporary tune.

"You shouldn't have had the passion fizz," Kaleb said, joining her at the railing.

They were alone; Helen and Essie had disappeared into the house.

Susan felt the nape of her neck prickle. "Why? Because I feel like humming? Not all of life is a harsh reality of barren valleys and desert plains, Mr. Kaleb Knight, *sir*. As your aunt said, life on Sapphire Island is soft and beautiful."

His voice was deep and spiked with irony. "In a manner of speaking, but even softness and beauty must face reality."

"Really? Well, I've never subscribed to the Royal Order of Cynics," Susan retorted with a toss of her head. She felt mean, hateful, spiteful toward this man who managed to twist everything she touched, thought or felt.

"The world is full of cynics," Kaleb intoned caustically. "They're the survivors. It's only young women like you, who have been sheltered like hot house blooms, who believe in a cocoon-wrapped world."

"You have a very clever tongue, Kaleb Knight, but

you'll never convince me the gates to heaven are paved with cynicism."

"I have no intention of trying to convince you of anything, Miss McRay. I have better things to do with my time."

His words were like a sharp slap, and Susan's anger billowed and frayed like a cloud before a storm. "As do I, Mr. Knight. Arguing with you is rather pointless. The night is much too beautiful to waste." She returned to her surveillance of the stars and velvety dark sky, the night calls of a thousand and one birds.

The moon was climbing behind the palms, casting a silvery glow. It was truly lovely, and she refused to let the presence of one Kaleb Knight ruin it for her. She took a sip of brandy and raised her chin to the gentle breeze.

"Flippant little hellcat tonight, aren't you?" He sounded cold with control.

"Hellcat?" she queried as coolly. "Does that parallel the jungle jaguar who stalks its prey and then pounces without warning? If so, I'm flattered. A jaguar is a sleek, sophisticated animal of incredible intelligence. Always wary, always alert...As I must be in defense of your arrogance, black moods, and self-assured sarcasm. I've never met a man like you before. You are insufferable."

"It's not surprising that you think so, considering your minimal experience," Kaleb barbed. "One love affair doesn't classify you as an expert. Shall we drink to that?" He raised his glass, amusement flickering in his eyes.

"Why not?" she responded, matching his tone. "I may not be an expert, but at least I have feelings and the ability to care, qualities you've obviously lost along your tangled path of cynicism. And I'll drink to that!"

Susan realized she was trembling, and to her horror didn't know if it was from her barely-controlled anger or the nearness of the maddening man who had suddenly stepped closer—until there was barely the width of a hand between them.

"Steady," he drawled, sensing her dilemma and, she had no doubt, proposing to take full advantage of it.

Everything about the man had sharp edges, cutting away at her as he toyed with her emotions. The moon had climbed higher, casting his face in ominous shadow, but she could feel the green sparks in his eyes consuming her until time seemed to stand still.

"Beneath my crusty shell of cynicism and cold arrogance there beats a heart just like any other, my teinetiti. And there also lie passionate urges."

"We've discussed this subject before," Susan said, barely above a whisper. She could feel the warmth of him, and the pain of her pounding heart.

"So we have, but not to my satisfaction. The little innocents of the world, like yourself, are the ones who travel the fairy tale train of make-believe, unaware they have passions as well."

She backed away, clutching the fragile stem of her glass. "Why do you insist on being so unpleasant?" she choked, her inner turmoil complete. "Yesterday, we shared our past as friends—and shared as well some of the magic of the island. Now, we're enemies. I refuse to spend three weeks in paradise turned hell because of conflicting personalities and the damnable hostility you can't seem to keep in check. Nor should

I have to keep two feet ahead of you to ward off your advances!" Her breath was coming in short gasps and her pulse raced. Oh, why didn't he just leave? Why didn't he fly away to his silver mine in Arizona and leave her to the peace and serenity of the island!

"Friendship is a rather complicated word," he reasoned, stepping close once again—so close, his warm breath fanned her face. "Friendship can only be maintained when two people like each other." He reached out and stroked her cheek, and his touch was surprisingly gentle. "Though you'll have to admit we have something going between us."

When he bent his head, Susan froze. He was going to kiss her again!

But he was as unpredictable as a summer storm. His kiss was brief, light, and on her forehead. "You can open your eyes now, Miss McRay," came his voice turned velvety smooth. "Unless you'd rather I didn't see those eyes of yours flecked with the purple passion of desire."

The amused arrogance in his tone struck Susan like a physical blow. His indifferent kiss had been more devastating to her than a kiss on the mouth. He was laughing at her, mocking her because he knew only too well the effect of his lips, his touch. She had sworn he would never take advantage of her again, yet again she had been betrayed by her own body.

Her cheeks were still flushed when she raised her eyes to his. Oh, how correct she had been in her first evaluation of him! "You have a strong arm and a long blade on your knife, Mr. Knight, and your heart is made of stone."

His eyes slipped over her and a dimple flashed.

"Why so dramatic, love? You spoke of friendship. Wouldn't you consider that a friendly kiss?"

"It might as well have been a slap in the face," Susan lashed out at him, "for it wasn't given out of friendship. Now, if you'll excuse me, I, too, have better things to do with my time."

She escaped into the moonlit night, fuming all the way to the tree house.

CHAPTER
Seven

IT HAD NEVER occurred to Susan that there would come a time in her life when she would feel so unsettled, when the night would seem a million years long. Even after her fiery breakup with Paul, she'd managed a few dreamless, restful nights. But now it was a different matter entirely. Her dreams were erotic, sensual, frightening—and full of Kaleb Knight. They left her feeling limp. How, she wondered, could she find a way to douse the flames of her desire for him when even her dreams betrayed her?

The light of early dawn pressing against her eyelids, Susan blinked and rolled wearily from bed. Today Essie and Helen were leaving for Tutuila. She would miss them even though she hadn't seen much of them. Maybe she should have gone along. Would Kaleb's maddening moods be even worse with his mother and aunt away? She had dreaded the day she would have to leave the island, but now she was actually looking forward to it. Her tiny apartment in San Francisco seemed an inviting oasis of security.

After a breakfast of toast, coffee, and sweet melon, Susan dressed in white shorts and a tiny yellow halter, and tied her hair up in yellow yarn. Her newly acquired tan looked golden in the morning light. At least she would return to San Francisco with enviable color.

Sipping a second cup of coffee on the veranda, she became lost in thought. The island was an artist's dream. The lagoon, the stately palms, the ocean beyond. Even the tree house itself would be an appropriate subject. Still, at this moment none of it appealed to her.

She considered making the village and Laelia's sister and uncle subjects for a painting, but Kaleb had forbidden her to go there alone. A smile tugged at the corners of her pink mouth. Kaleb Knight wasn't her keeper. If she decided to go to the village, she would! She would talk to Sam about it. Surely he wouldn't disapprove, and he might even help her select a horse for the venture. With that thought came the grand idea for her first subject—the gray stallion, Moonflight. Now *that* was exciting!

The sun was creeping up over the palms when Susan reached the stable. Surprised but happy to see Sam there feeding and watering the horses, she waved. He looked magnificent in faded blue jeans, barechested, with trim hips and muscular biceps.

"I'd like to do a painting of you one day soon," Susan said, joining him as he moved toward the exercise ring. "Though I'd rather have you in one of those Samoan skirts."

"It's called a lava-lava," Sam smiled. "I wear it most of the time, but when I work with the horses or in the garden, I find Mr. Kaleb's western pants more suitable. You're up very early this morning, Miss Susan."

She nodded. "Did Helen and Essie get off okay? I said good-bye to them at dinner last night."

"The seaplane left at six-thirty, Miss Susan. There was much excitement. Miss Essie couldn't find her reading glasses, and Miss Helen had misplaced her white shawl."

Susan laughed, picturing it.

It was already quite warm, and she didn't want to keep Sam from his chores. "I'd like to do some sketches of Moonflight, Sam. Would it be possible to bring him out?"

He nodded agreeably. "Would you like him in the exercise yard or tethered to a tree?"

"In the exercise ring, I think. He's such a magnificent animal, I'd like to try and capture him as he should be, wild and free."

Sam went for the stallion, and Susan climbed up on the railing carrying a sketch pad and pencil. If she was working with a landscape, seascape, or still life, she would plunge right in with paint and brush, but with a portrait study, human or animal, she preferred to make sketches first.

Sam led the stallion into the exercise ring and closed the gate. "He'll get spoiled if you take too long," Sam teased. "He'll think he's special."

"He is special, Sam. I've never seen anything so beautiful. Look at the way his muscles ripple, and the color! He shines like sterling silver in the sunlight. Did Mr. Knight breed him along with the others?"

"He carries this Arabian stock on his ranch in Arizona," Sam volunteered, joining her on the rail. "A very long time ago the only way to get to our village was on foot or by canoe up the river. When Mr. Kade took sick, Mr. Kaleb shipped stock from the United States and built the stable." •

"Does Laelia ride?" Susan asked.

"She rides the mare you were on yesterday, Miss Susan."

"And would the mare be a good choice if I decided to ride to the village by myself? I'd like to do some sketches of Luina as well as Mutu at work." She held her breath, waiting for his response.

"The mare would be a good choice." His white teeth flashed. He looked pleased that she was interested in his people.

"You think I can make the trip on my own then?"

Sam's warm brown eyes met hers. "Do *you* think you can make the trip on your own?"

"It didn't seem difficult following along behind Mr. Knight."

"It isn't. The pathway is difficult to follow in only two places, but if you observed the pathway yesterday, you should do well."

Relieved—at least Sam didn't think she was a headstrong idiot—Susan began to sketch. Sam watched for a while, and then went about his duties. She became engrossed in her work, enthralled with every movement the stallion made. It was almost as though he knew what she was doing and was putting on a show for her benefit. The proud head held high, the toss of his sweeping mane, the arch of his long neck—he was gorgeous!

After completing a second sketch, Susan moved to a spot along the rail in the shade of a Pandanas tree, in no hurry to get back to work. In a few moments, her subject trotted over to where she sat and nudged her leg with his nose.

"You're so lovely," Susan crooned, rubbing his silky neck. "You know I like you, don't you?" Nostrils flared as he raised his head, nickering softly, almost intimately. His alert eyes watched Susan's every move, and even warned her of approaching footsteps before she heard them.

It was Sam, carrying a thermos, old army blanket, and a paper sack. "Coffee break," he grinned. "Isn't that what you call it in America?"

Susan laughed and nodded. Sam helped her down, and they shared the blanket in the shade of the tree. He reached into his pocket and took out a few pieces of carrot. "For you to give to Moonflight," he said, "though I think you have already won him over."

"He knows I admire him, that's all." She showed Sam the sketches. They were good, but there was one she liked in particular. She'd managed to catch the stallion at just the right angle. Sam exclaimed over the drawings, picking out her favorite, too. "That's the one I'll paint," she told him.

From the paper sack, Sam extracted hard-boiled eggs, cheese, slices of coffee cake, and two bananas. Delighted by the idea of a spontaneous picnic, Susan tossed her head and laughed. "Sam, you think of everything!"

"Laelia is the one who has thought of everything,

Miss Susan. She left enough prepared food to feed the island for a week." His brown eyes clouded over. "But most of it will go to waste if Mr. Kaleb continues to hibernate."

Susan's hand, on the way to her mouth, stopped in mid-air. "Mr. Knight isn't eating?" she queried hesitantly.

"No, but it is not unusual. When he is at work, a day or two days will sometimes pass before he thinks of food."

"And—And is he at work now?"

"Yes. In the study room. He has been typing since his mother and aunt left this morning."

Sternly reminding herself that Kaleb Knight wasn't her concern, that he was his own keeper and a rather offensive one at that, Susan concentrated on Sam, a much more pleasant subject. "Do you have a girl friend, Sam?" she asked.

He brightened, his brown eyes aglow. "In Pago Pago. She teaches at the college."

"How difficult for you! How on earth do you manage to get together?"

"On my days off I sometimes fly to Tutuila. When we marry she will come to Sapphire Island and teach the children in the village."

"And when will that be?"

"As soon as I have saved enough money to build a house. My land is near the river. It is very beautiful."

"And Laelia. Does she have a boy friend?"

"Laelia's husband was killed in a storm last year, Miss Susan. They had only been married a few weeks. We haven't the storms of the other islands, but occasionally we do get one that breaks open the sky.

Kei was on the beach when it struck. A tree fell, crushing him."

Susan found herself trembling. "My God, how awful!"

"Our island holds many joys and is very beautiful, but it can sometimes be cruel. More coffee?"

Susan held out her mug for a refill, but Sam's words had hit home. Even in paradise the harsh realities of life intruded. Was that what Kaleb had tried to tell her?

"You are far away, Miss Susan, and your face is sad. Don't let my words lower your spirit. There is much to be happy for, and the sun is warm. Come. I will show you Sunbird, Moonflight's bride. She is due with foal soon."

Thankful for Sam's perception, she followed him into the stable to a separate stall where a golden Arabian contentedly munched on oats.

"She is due within the week. You will be able to see the youngster before you leave the island. It is Moonflight's first offspring, and Mr. Kaleb is very excited."

"As he well should be," Susan said softly. "He managed to bring a little of the Arizona desert to paradise, didn't he? She's a beautiful mare."

"He has also managed to take a part of our island to Arizona and the western world in the books he writes. He is much like his father. He gives of himself until one must wonder what there is left to give. But there always seems to be more."

The strange feeling of not really knowing Kaleb Knight swept over her. She gave a soft sigh of regret. She would never know him. But no matter where she went, she would carry within her the sights and sounds, the eternal beauty, of Sapphire Island.

"You're not describing the man I know as Kaleb Knight," Susan told him. "One minute Mr. Knight seems to care and is friendly and the next, it's as though he can't tolerate me. It doesn't make any sense." She flushed, color mounting as well as her pulse rate. It wasn't her place to discuss Kaleb or his hangups with Sam, but she felt she must tell someone, and she considered Sam a friend.

"What in life does make sense?" Sam asked. "Can anyone say why we do a certain thing? Mr. Kaleb is not a man of stone, as you might think. He is like the hawk who flies in search of his mate. Until the day comes when he finds her, he will shower those around him with a rain of anger." Sam broke off, lowering his eyes as if realizing it wasn't his place to discuss Kaleb Knight with a virtual stranger.

Susan reached out and touched his arm. "We can change the subject if talking about Mr. Knight makes you uncomfortable, Sam, but you're wrong. Mr. Knight is not searching for a mate. His broken romance has left him bitter. He doesn't believe in love."

"All men must seek a mate," Sam responded soundly. "The heart will heal as time passes, and life will look different. He will know this one day, and then he will be happy again."

"In the meantime, he has a place to mend his heart like no other, Sam. Men spend their lives dreaming about an island such as this. I wonder if Mr. Knight knows how lucky he really is."

Sam gave her a lopsided grin. "The magic of the island is in your eyes, Miss Susan."

She nodded wistfully. "I'm afraid so. I must be one of those people you talked about that first day, remember? 'There are those who come and want to stay,' you said. Unfortunately, I can't stay, and it's also unfortunate I'm such a silly romantic." She picked up her sketch pad and pencil. Sam sat in good light, and she couldn't think of a better time to do a sketch of him.

"You need a prettier subject," he teased when he realized what she was doing.

"What I need is you. Right now, at this very moment, my friend. I need your strength and your kindness. Now sit still!"

Soon the sketch was finished, and when Susan showed it to Sam, he whipped his head back in laughter. "That cannot be me. This man on paper is a handsome man who has lights dancing in his eyes."

"You are handsome, Sam, and I do see lights dancing in your eyes."

"Then you must allow me to draw you as I see you, Miss Susan."

Susan's mouth opened in surprise as he reached for the sketch pad and pencil. "You're an artist?"

The chuckle came from deep in his throat. "No, Miss Susan, but I like to draw."

Deftly he worked without uttering a sound, and when he was finished, Susan gasped with delight. It wasn't just a head study, but all of her. Her arms were stretched out, her long legs crossed, her head tossed back. It was good! Even though it flattered her. "You *are* an artist!" she exclaimed. "Have you ever thought about painting? Working with colors on canvas?"

When he shook his head, looking embarrassed, she

hurried on. "Would you like to try it? We could get together some afternoon and have a real fling at it. Please, Sam, say yes!"

"How could I refuse your excitement." Sam smiled. "It would be fun."

It was late afternoon before Susan finally made her way back to the tree house. Feeling relaxed, she took a refreshing shower, shrugged into a wisp of a dressing gown, and prepared a light dinner. While a tray of package biscuits baked in the oven, she took a glass of white wine with ice out to the veranda, kicked off her sandals, and stretched out in a chair. Sam, she decided, had given her this feeling of euphoria. He was a special friend, and she had enjoyed the day immensely. Even now, though she was alone with her thoughts and away from his magic influence, she still felt a sense of well-being. She had done the sketches she wanted and found a new star pupil. His talent had been a delightful surprise, but then everything about the day had been inspiring.

Sinking further into the wicker chair, she breathed deeply. It was a beautiful evening. The nearby jungle seemed alive with birds whose chorus of songs filled the air, which was heavy with the scents of sweet-smelling ginger and frangipani.

She was deep in thought, planning what colors to use on the painting of Moonflight, when one of Kaleb's green birds swooped between the trees and finally came to rest on her shoulder. It was Tasi, and Susan's heart stopped. She doubted that the bird had come on her own.

As if in answer to her thought, Kaleb appeared, handsome in russet slacks and a creamy silk shirt. He leaned against the trellis leading to the veranda and lifted a brow. "I knocked, so don't think of me as a bold intruder. Besides, I sent my emissary on ahead. Something smells good."

"B-biscuits," Susan stammered, springing to life. Why was she always so tongue-tied around this maddening man? "Just out of the oven."

"I expected you to come to the house for dinner," Kaleb drawled, his green eyes roaming over her at a leisurely pace. He missed no detail—her golden tan, her head of chestnut curls, the rapid rise and fall of her breasts beneath the sheer fabric of her gown, her bare feet and painted toes.

"I preferred the solitude of the tree house tonight," she said thickly, wondering why it mattered anyway. Just because he chose to come out of his hole...

"Is that my cue to leave?"

If she said yes, he *would* leave and that would be the end of it. She resented his intrusion, but did she truly want him to leave?

"While you're debating, I'll fix myself a drink. May I freshen yours?"

"Just white wine," she said, handing her glass to him.

"And one ice cube. A rather interesting way to drink a glass of wine." He headed for the kitchen via the veranda, but not before Susan caught the amusement tugging at the corners of his mouth. Damn him! So adding ice to white wine wasn't accepted in a better guide to bartending. It was *her* way, and he didn't need to make a sport of it.

Tasi had moved to a tree branch, and sat preening her feathers. "You have an infuriating master, my little friend," Susan muttered in aggravation. "Too bad his disposition doesn't match his good looks."

Taking several deep breaths, and remembering her determination to douse cold water on the smoldering fire of her desire, she arranged her gown around her and counted to ten. Then twenty. The gown was revealing, especially since the uninvited guest was Kaleb Knight. But to change into something more suitable now would only add to his amusement.

When Kaleb returned, he took a seat opposite Susan, and then leaned close, handing her the glass of wine. "You look lovely tonight, Miss McRay," he said huskily. "That's a very pretty gown. I can see you've acquired more sun along the way." His eyes took in the inviting cleavage just above the first button.

Was he teasing or serious? She couldn't tell, but her skin tingled.

"By the way, the biscuits are done. I took the liberty of removing them from the oven and covering them with a towel. Let me know the next time you crave biscuits and I'll teach you to make them from scratch."

Susan groaned and looked out at the night, not bothering to respond. She didn't care what he thought. She sipped the wine, savoring the feel of it along her parched throat. The night sounds crept in, enveloping her. He had moved closer still. She could feel his warm breath on her shoulder.

"Will you forgive me for last night? I behaved like an idiot. That's one of the reasons I'm here, to ask you to forgive me."

He wasn't teasing. Susan could see the sincerity in his face, hear it in his voice. "And the other reason?" she asked, just above a whisper.

"I wanted to share the solitude of the night, Susan. It's a night for lovers."

"But we aren't lovers, Kaleb. We aren't even friends. I wanted to be your friend, but you managed to destroy that relationship before it began."

She met his eyes, glittering green, and the blaze of white teeth, though his smile was brief. "I don't blame you for being angry, but I'm only human and you're very lovely. If I promise to keep my red-blooded feelings to myself and a civil tongue in my head, can we call a truce?"

Susan searched his face, and finding only open friendliness, nodded. Would she ever understand him?

He bent swiftly to place a chaste kiss on her cheek. "Good! Now would you like to have company for dinner?" He leaned back in his chair and smiled. His dimples creased his cheeks so appealingly that Susan found herself responding.

"You haven't eaten?" she asked.

"I'm afraid my appetite went out the door with our friendship. You have a strong hold over my gangly frame, my love. Did I notice tuna salad in the frig?"

How could she refuse? "There's enough for two, but the biscuits are probably cold by now."

"Then we'll pop open another tin and have another drink!" He pulled her up, wrapped an arm around her waist, and propelled her into the kitchen, where the beautifully carved table was set for two, complete with Helen's china, silver, and an orchid centerpiece.

Dumbfounded, Susan cried out with pleasure. "You did all this while you were fixing our drinks?"

"I'm full of surprises, love," he teased, popping the cork on a bottle of champagne that had been chilling in ice. Ceremoniously, he poured the bubbling liquid into two crystal goblets. With unexpected tenderness he said, "If Mohammed won't come to the mountain... I appreciate sharing my beautiful island with someone who loves it almost as much as I do, Susan, and I'm not wrong, am I? You have grown to love it. I can see it in your eyes."

"Y-yes." Her voice was husky with emotion. "You're full of surprises Kaleb Knight. I'll never truly understand you, not if I have an entire lifetime."

"I'm like those stones of time, my teinetiti. It would take a lifetime to turn them all over. Most of the time, I don't understand what I'm all about myself. I only know it's important to set the record straight, and I can do that best by proposing a toast." He raised his glass into the air.

"'No one will ever live long enough to enjoy eternal paradise,'" he said, "'but if one must try, at least give him truth and beauty if only for a moment...' To that I'll add, at this very moment, I have enough truth and beauty to last me that lifetime."

They touched glasses while Susan fought down the lump clogging her throat. "Th-that was beautiful, Kaleb."

"So it's 'Kaleb' again, is it? Well, I suppose that proves you've accepted my apology. Shall we check on the biscuits?"

By the time they'd baked another tin and Susan had added a few additional ingredients to the salad to make it stretch for two, they were on their second glass of champagne and at peace with the world as well as themselves.

"This might be a bit too romantic for a friendly dinner," Kaleb offered, lighting two candle tapers, "but if we both know and understand where we're coming from..."

But the question was, did she? She wasn't at all certain, but she wouldn't have exchanged the magic of the moment for a million tomorrows.

"Penny for your thoughts?" Kaleb asked, his green eyes watching her intently.

Susan sat down, drawing a napkin across her lap. "As I recall, you asked me that once before, remember?"

"Hmmmm, and what was your reply?"

"That I was thinking how difficult you are to understand."

"And is that what you're thinking now?"

"Yes. And how difficult it's going to be to leave. Despite all the headaches you've given me, I've managed to enjoy almost every moment."

"Almost?" Green flames flickered over her face.

"Well, I haven't appreciated the hours we've been at odds with one another."

A dimple creased his cheek. "We do seem to spark a fire when we're together, don't we?"

Susan felt herself relax. "That, my friend, is an understatement."

"Then let's make a pact, love. No more headaches or fires burning out of control. Deal?"

Susan nodded, taking his extended hand.

The biscuits were golden and hot and the salad cool and crisp, and after Kaleb had eaten his last bite, he smiled with contentment. "If the salad is a representative example of your cooking, I think you might be able to teach me a thing or two about preparing biscuits from scratch."

Having eaten more than she had in days, Susan sighed, equally content. "You could say I'm a woman of many talents. I made my first sketches today."

"Ah, so that's where you've been. Out sketching the tree tops and pounding surf. I came by earlier."

"As a matter of fact, I was at the stables sketching Moonflight and Sam," Susan told him, draining her coffee cup. "Both make excellent subjects. The sketches are in the living room if you'd care to see them."

Kaleb took her hand as she led him into the living room. Spotting the sketch of her, he asked, "And is that a self-portrait?"

"Oh, no!" she responded. "That's Sam's contribution. He's really quite good. I'm going to give him some lessons in oils."

The change in Kaleb came immediately and without warning. His brows furrowed and his jaw tightened. "Is that what you were wearing?"

Too surprised at his reaction to think clearly, she nodded. "Shorts and a halter. Is there something wrong?"

"I don't think it's a wise idea to go around dressed like that, Susan. Especially in front of Sam."

She couldn't believe her ears. "Shorts and a halter?" she queried. "My God, Kaleb, this isn't exactly the dark ages, and Sam is hardly Jack the Ripper!"

"Even so, it's the kind of an outfit to turn a man into something he's not. Sam may be no more than a Samoan native in your eyes, but he's a man, after all, and could get ideas if you continue to parade about half naked."

Susan stiffened as if a jolt of electricity had shot through her body. Just as suddenly, cold anger washed over her like a giant tidal wave, merciless in its attack. "If you consider wearing shorts and a halter 'parading about half naked,' then I must be nude this very minute. Shorts and a halter aren't nearly as revealing as this dressing gown. And after all, you, too, are a mortal man, Kaleb Knight, are you not?"

He studied her silently his eyes moving over her face, long neck, and bare shoulders.

Susan's violet eyes, now dark purple in their rage, were fixed on the handsome figure before her. All his sugar and sweet talk about friendship was a ruse to get back in her good graces. And what for? So he could open up all the wounds he'd originally inflicted?

His eyes softened a bit and he looked flustered, as though he'd just come aground after a long trip at sea. But she didn't care. Once again, he'd managed to ruin a beautiful evening. When was she going to learn?

"Susan—" He broke off, rubbing his eyes.

"Don't you 'Susan' me. I should have realized you are the same despicable person you've always been. The devil craves his sorcery, destroying everything beautiful, and that's what you've done! You've taken innocence and turned it into lechery. You've taken friendship and made a mockery of the word."

His slightly flustered look was gone. Now he appeared formidable. Alert, dangerous, hardened, and capable of God only knew what. "If you're going to be childish about this, I've proven my point. You're so damned naive you couldn't see the writing on the wall if it was in ten-foot letters. Well, you'd better wake up, young lady, because if you don't, it's going to be too late!"

"Too late for what?" Susan challenged, desperately trying to control the urge to slug him. "To save my virginity? Well, that flew the coop when I thought I'd found my loving partner for life. I gave Paul my virginity and you my friendship, and in both cases I've been slapped in the face. For your information, Sam Kahanakee is ten times the man you or Paul could ever hope to be. He's kind, considerate, and understanding."

"And he has a girl on Tutuila. Did he tell you that?"

"Of course he told me, and I won't let you ruin their relationship or my friendship with Sam with your lousy accusations. Now get out while I can still think and act like a lady. I'm sorry, but it *hasn't* been fun!"

"Because you're a child," he flung at her. "Is this your coup de grâce, this nightly display of temper? Why are you being such a fool!"

He caught her wrist in his viselike grip and she cried out in pain. There was no tenderness in him now. His mouth came down on hers in an assault that sent panic jolting through her. She kicked and struggled, but she was powerless in his hard embrace.

It was Kaleb who finally broke away, but not until she had gone limp in his arms, defeated by desire. She wanted his arms around her, yearned for his lips on her flesh. She longed for his love with a driving hunger she dared not admit. She was leaning against him, moaning, almost begging him, like a woman possessed.

Consuming her with eyes grown dark with passion, he reached out and unbuttoned her gown.

"No!" she heard herself cry. But it was a pitiful cry without meaning. It was one thing to vow a million and one promises to herself when apart, but quite another matter when he held her in his arms. What black magic did he hold over her? And what could she do to break the spell? "I hate you," she muttered feebly.

Again she was crushed against his chest, but when his mouth met hers this time, his lips were tender, probing, demanding her breath from her body, the essence from her soul. Her hands pulled at the buttons on his shirt, tangled with the curly hair that grew like a russet mat on his chest and then slipped around to where his back and shoulder muscles rippled with every movement.

He pulled her down to the rug. She didn't try to escape. Every nerve in her body cried out for fulfillment. Her bare breasts rose and fell as he kissed each pink-tipped mound. His hands caressed the vulnerable spots and then caressed them again. She was powerless to resist, but not because of some black magic. She loved him, and the truth washed over her, consuming her completely. She had never felt like this with Paul, yet she had thought she loved him. Fool that she was!

Roughly then, Kaleb pulled away, wrenching himself from her body with an agonized breath. He struggled to his feet, pulling her up beside him. "Now if that wasn't lust, what was it?" he retorted dryly. "You're so quick to condemn, but at the slightest hint of physical contact with 'mortal man,' as you so caustically put it, you go soft and pliant and more than willing. Well, my dear young lady, you won't seduce Sam Kahanakee. I'll see to that!"

At that moment, Susan could have proclaimed her love for him, but she knew he wouldn't believe her. He was convinced she meant to seduce Sam Kahanakee, absurd though the idea was. And even if he did believe her, he could offer nothing in return. Kaleb's ice-coated heart would not be given away again. He had made that clear at the onset.

Still angry in defeat, she rebuttoned her gown and strode to the door. "Get out," she choked, "and don't come back."

There wasn't a flicker of emotion in his steady gaze. "Don't worry. I'll stay away from you, but only if you stay away from Sam. If you don't, I'll be back. You can count on it!"

He shut the door soundly, and tears filled her eyes. How could she love him and hate him at the same time? Was she mad?

On soundless feet, she ran to the bedroom and fell full length on the bed. She lay there a long time listening to the night sounds of the jungle and the beating of her heart. She trembled when she remembered the feel of Kaleb's arms, the taste of his lips. What would become of her? She had fallen in love with Satan himself.

CHAPTER
Eight

LIGHT WAS STREAKING in from the east when Susan reached the stable the following morning. She'd tossed and turned half the night, and finally, unable to tolerate one more moment of torment, had defiantly donned blue jeans and the tiniest halter she owned and fled into the morning stillness.

The sky was just beginning to lighten, but the air was already warm. Samoan fantails fluttered through the trees, and a great reef heron swooped down in search of breakfast. Beauty surrounded her, but she was numb to it. If only she could lose herself in her art work. But would it be enough?

Entering the stable, Susan checked on Sunbird, patted the gentle mare she'd ridden to the village, and smiled in spite of her mood when Moonflight kicked up a fuss at the sound of her voice. "Jealous, are you," she crooned, stroking his elegant neck. "Maybe a whirl around the exercise ring will calm you down."

It wasn't until she'd opened his stall to lead him to the ring that the thought occurred to her. He'd met her with gentle nudges of affection, almost taunting her to ride him, and her heart skipped a beat. Did she dare? Well, why not—if he would allow it. She could try him in the ring and then. . . . Her heart soared as high as the great reef heron. The thought of riding Moonflight along the beach and possibly beyond—maybe to the village—consumed her with excitement. She needed to escape, to fly like the wind. She needed this great horse beneath her—his power and grace and affection.

"Well," she said softly, "will you be agreeable or a devil like your Master?" The horse nudged her again and nickered softly. "I take that to mean you're agreeable," she laughed, "so let's give it a try!"

Tethering Moonflight to a post and then dragging a sheepskin and saddle from the tack room, she worked carefully and calmly until both were in place on the great stallion's back. Giving the cinch a final tug—the saddle was beautifully hand tooled—and with the determination of the damned, she swung up into the saddle. The animal flicked its ears, nickered again, and moved at her command. Giddy with delight, she leaned over and gave him a hug. There was no need to waste time in the ring. Moonflight was her friend and would give her a good ride without difficulty.

Once on the beach, Susan relaxed, molding herself to the saddle as she'd been taught long ago. She had left a note for Sam tacked to Moonflight's stall, and she prayed he would find it, and not Kaleb. Sam would understand, but Kaleb would be irate. Not that it mattered. She had suffered a sleepless night, but was now more determined than ever. Kaleb Knight would never touch her again, physically or emotionally.

The sun was up, breaking through the palms, by the time Susan reached the river. Turning inland, she talked to her beautiful gray mount, relishing the feel of him beneath her, caught up in the beauty of the island coming to life around her. The sun cast its rays through the trees, a brilliant shaft of light from heaven to earth. Birds of every description soared overhead, swooping across the river.

She skirted a pond, remembering that, just beyond, the path became lost amid a tangle of vines. Carefully watching for the place, she picked up the path further on. She'd had time to notice many details on her previous ride, since her companion had been so silent and glum. Fleetingly, she wondered if Kaleb's broken romance had soured him on life and the female sex, or if he had always been hateful. She was more inclined to believe his cursedness was as much a part of him as leaves on a tree. If so, no woman would ever be safe with him.

Scolding herself for dwelling on what she couldn't change, Susan cleared her mind with a healthy shake of her chestnut curls and forged ahead, only stopping beside a bubbling brook for a ten-minute rest.

It was mid-morning when she reached the village. Giggling children and barking dogs welcomed her. Men and women waved, and Chief Fua appeared as she dismounted.

"Talofa, Miss Susan," he beamed, extending his hand. "This is a surprise."

Susan took the old man's hand and returned his smile. "Talofa, Chief Fua. I hope I'm not intruding."

"This is your home while you are on our island," he responded. "You are tired after your ride. You must rest and take food."

Tuai, Luina's husband, strode over from a neighboring fale, and, smiling at Susan, whispered something in the chief's ear.

"Tuai says his wife is not feeling well, but you are welcome to join the family meal."

The wise old man didn't question Susan about her solo arrival, and, as before, she felt totally welcome.

In the fale, family members were gathered in groups. Susan sat among them, accepting bowls of baked bananas, biscuits, and yams. Luina looked pale, but she smiled and joined Susan on the woven mat.

Concerned, Susan asked, "Have you been ill? Your husband said you aren't feeling well."

"I am all right, Miss Susan. My husband worries too much. He must fish today and regrets having to leave me. It is near time for the baby. Another week, maybe two..."

Nuta, Luina's mother, handed Susan a cup of orange leaf tea and smiled. "My Laelia is with Miss Helen on Tutuila, but she will return in time for the birth."

"And then Laelia will be an aunt." Susan smiled. "It's an exciting time when there's a new baby."

"Time for much celebration," Nuta nodded. She studied Susan's face. "You are on Samala's horse. Is he all right?"

Susan felt her cheeks flush, wondering what these

dear people would think if she admitted to taking Sam's horse without permission. "He's fine, Nuta. We spent the afternoon together just yesterday, as a matter of fact. He's a very good artist. That's what I do for a living, teach art, and I'd like to give him a few lessons on how to paint with oil before I leave."

They seemed impressed, so Susan went on. "That's one of the reasons I'm here this morning. I'd like to do some sketches of Luina as well as Mutu while he's at work. Would that be possible?"

Luina laughed and lowered her head. "You want to draw me?"

"Oh, yes!" Susan exclaimed. "You have a beautiful face. You would make a lovely painting."

"And old Mutu," Nuta teased. "Would his painting be lovely, too?"

"He's a darling, and he would make a different kind of subject," Susan responded.

"I'd like to be in your picture," Luina replied.

"Good! Perhaps we could go somewhere close by after breakfast . . . if you feel up to it. I'd like a beautiful setting where you could pose comfortably. Something secluded."

"Near the water," Luina volunteered. "It isn't far. I go there almost every morning to look for shells. I make ulasisis—necklaces to be sold in Pago Pago. Many of our offerings are sent there to be sold. We receive our farming supplies in return. Mr. Kaleb would rather give us our supplies without worry of sales on Tutuila, but we pay our own way. Do you like the masi . . . biscuits?"

Susan nodded. "They're delicious."

"They are made from breadfruit. I will show you how to make them and then you can surprise Mr.

Kaleb with your knowledge."

"Mr. Kaleb and I are at odds, I'm afraid," Susan said truthfully. "I doubt I'll be seeing much of him between now and the time I leave."

Nuta shook her head. "Mr. Kaleb is a kind and gentle man, but he must be loved to be understood." Her brown eyes danced.

Had these perceptive people picked up the truth already? Did her love for him show?

Susan sighed. "Even when he's loved, he's impossible to understand." There was little reason to conceal the truth when they knew it anyway. "He can be gentle, kind, considerate, and beautiful, but he can also bring heartbreak and despair. He is both a jungle cat and a stubborn mule. His moods change with the tide and as swiftly as the river. I can not accustom myself to all those up and down emotions, and I'm no longer going to try."

The women exchanged knowing glances, and dropped the subject.

After the meal, Luina led the way to a beach at the southern end of the island where the shoreline was gentle and the breeze a mere whisper. The sand was as soft and white as spun sugar, and flowers grew in masses, cascading over and under the trees and spilling out onto the sand.

"I can see by your face that you like what you see," Luina said. "To the left, you can see the reef. Perhaps you flew over it before landing on the water."

"Yes, and is it also where your village fishes by torchlight?"

Luina nodded. "That is a treat you must join before you leave our island, Miss Susan. One week away, and we will fish for sea bass for our fia fia, our monthly feast. You will be here for that, too. The village will welcome you."

It sounded like a delightful experience, one she wouldn't miss. "Now, where can you sit so you can be comfortable?" she asked, hoping this wouldn't be too strenuous for the girl in her condition.

"In the sand with my back against a palm. This is exciting. I have never been a model before."

"You know about modeling then?" Susan was surprised.

"I went to school on Tutuila for a year, Miss Susan. I learned much."

"Then others from the village have gone to school too?"

Luina nodded. "In the beginning, Mr. Kade taught us about the outside world, but later he made arrangements on Tutuila. When Samala's bride comes to live on the island, she will teach the children here."

"I know. Sam told me. He seems very much in love with her."

"He is, Miss Susan. She is very beautiful. It would be nice if you could meet her."

"A lot of things would be nice." Susan sighed wistfully.

Settled and relatively comfortable, she began to sketch, thrilling to the girl's natural beauty and the ease with which she managed to capture it on paper. She would do two paintings and give one to Luina as a gift.

Susan was on the second sketch when Luina doubled over and moaned. Her dark skin had developed a gray cast and a sheen of perspiration. Susan was by her side in an instant. "What is it, honey? Are you ill?"

Luina's eyes grew round in her lovely face. "The

baby, I think. I'm having a pain in my stomach." She doubled over again, gasping for breath.

Susan closed her eyes, forcing herself to think clearly. There was no one around, and they were five, maybe ten minutes from the village. Screams would only be heard by the birds. Tuai and the other men were fishing in a cove further down, but reaching them would take longer than racing to the village.

"Are the contractions strong? Are they too strong for you to move?"

Luina nodded. "I've been having them all morning," she admitted, "but they were little more than twinges. I thought they were what my mother calls false pains."

Lord, thought Susan, what had she gotten herself into? Did she dare leave the girl to seek help? Should they attempt to reach the village? From the look on Luina's pretty face, she decided either course would be too risky. The girl was in great pain, strangling on the cries threatening to rip from her throat.

Susan wasn't a nurse and had had no training in first aid, but she'd helped deliver a litter of puppies and a calf. Could it be much different? Probably a lot different! She took in great gulps of air, trying to calm down, then brushed Luina's damp hair from her forehead. "Do you think you can make it back to the village?"

"I think the baby is coming, Miss Susan. I—I can feel it. We have no time."

Thinking as quickly as her frantic mind would allow, Susan made a bed from the leaves of a banana tree and helped Luina stretch out. She then stripped off the girl's flowing puletasi and used it to cover her like a blanket. Beyond that, she could do little but wait.

Luina's breath was coming in short gasps now, in between her guttural groans, but her face radiated such wonder over what was about to happen that Susan found her own cheeks awash with tears. "Hang on, honey," she soothed. "You're going to be just fine. Soon, very soon, you're going to have a beautiful baby to hold in your arms."

Oh, how sure she sounded and how calm, when inside she was shaking like a leaf in a windstorm. The lull before the storm, thought Susan as Luina lay back and closed her eyes. Oh, why had she picked today of all days to come to the village? If it weren't for her, Luina would be safe at home having her baby. Capable hands would be tending her instead of her own inexperienced ones.

"You look worried, Miss Susan," Luina said softly. "Do not be afraid. I am glad you are here with me. It is good to have a friend to talk to." She smiled shyly. "It is too bad you are at odds with Mr. Kaleb. He needs a woman's loving arms to hold him and show him that life is beautiful. He needs a wife to give him a child." Her voice drifted off as once again pain lined her face. She gripped Susan's hand hard and cried out, her breath erupting from her throat.

And then time seemed to stop. Luina held her breath and then held it again as she bore down. As the sea sweeps the shore, every muscle in her body worked as one, and with a final grimace, the baby was expelled into Susan's waiting arms. When the tiny, wiggling creature cried out in protest, Susan's cheeks flooded with new tears. Luina lay back exhausted, but her eyes were bright.

"It's a boy," Susan breathed huskily. "It's a beautiful, healthy boy. Look, Luina! Oh, honey, look at him!"

Luina raised her head and her eyes held tears of joy as well. She reached out and touched his tiny fingers and toes. A new life had been born on Sapphire Island. Another stone had been turned.

It was a bedraggled Susan who stumbled into the village a short time later, her heart pounding with excitement. She found Nuta near the family fale. With one quick look at Susan, the woman nodded knowingly. "Is it too near time to bring her to the village?" she asked.

"The baby is here, Nuta!" Susan exclaimed. "It's a beautiful boy!"

Joy burst across Nuta's face, and other women joined in, gathering what they would need as Susan led the way to the beach. Everyone seemed to be talking at once in their own excited tongue, but when they reached the beach and found Luina snug on the banana leaves, with both she and the baby wrapped up in the colorful puletasi, their voices dissolved into awed whispers.

With everything under control, Susan collapsed under the nearest tree. Her hands were shaking as the full realization of what had happened finally hit her. The thrill of it was as sweet as anything she had ever known.

Soon Tuai arrived with two men carrying a litter. With infinite care, they transported Luina and her child back to the village, which was alive with excitement. Everyone wanted to celebrate the new birth, but Susan longed to rest and gather her thoughts. She headed toward Mutu's fale, where he was still hard at work putting the finishing touches on a beautiful cradle made of rich teak.

"Oh, it's for Luina's baby!" she exclaimed. "It's lovely!"

The old man's face creased with pleasure. "Yes, but I must hurry. The new child must have a bed."

Watching Muta hand-rub the rich wood, Susan didn't realize someone had entered the fale until a hand touched her shoulder. It was Tuai, and the smile on his face was as brilliant as a bright new morning. "Come," he said gently. "Luina would like to speak with you."

Susan followed him to where Luina was bedded down with her new son, who was contentedly nursing on one brown-tipped breast.

"I want to thank you for bringing my son into this world, Miss Susan," came her soft voice. "I can never repay you."

"You have a healthy son," Susan said wistfully, "and that's the only payment I need. Besides, you did all the work."

Luina laughed softly and kissed the top of the baby's head. "There will be much celebrating now. There always is when someone gives birth. Will you stay for the celebration?"

"I'd love to, if you don't think I'd be imposing."

"They will celebrate the birth, but they will honor our new friend as well, Miss Susan. You are one of us now."

Susan was touched by the girl's words, and as Luina rambled on, she began to sketch, wanting to capture the new mother's radiance. She worked for an hour drawing one sketch after another, aware of people coming and going to check on the newest addition to the village. When she finally put her sketch pad aside, both mother and child were fast asleep. Again someone touched Susan's shoulder. Nuta led her to the compound, where everyone seemed to be scurrying about, and explained that they would celebrate for three days. Food would be added to the food in the oven. Men would spear fish from the sea, and the children would gather flowers and water. The women would weave skirts of grass and create feathered headdresses as day followed day.

They had reached Chief Fua's fale, and he greeted them with a toothy smile, though it was Tuai who placed the orchid lei around Susan's neck, and announced that his newborn son would be named after her. "Ray for McRay," he told her amid the cheers of his people. "And someday, if we should be blessed with a daughter, we will name her Susan."

It was near dusk when Susan arrived at the stable. Although she was exhausted, the day had been one she would never forget.

She found Sam in the tack room, and when he saw her his face lit up. "Did you get my note?" she asked, dropping into a chair.

His brown eyes became guarded. "Yes, Miss Susan. I knew you would do well on Moonflight. But Mr. Kaleb—"

"Expected the crazy horse to toss you in the river," Kaleb finished for him. He stood in the doorway, his hands on his hips and his green eyes sparkling. "I worked all day, so I wasn't aware of your irresponsible stunt until half an hour ago. I've already given Sam hell for not letting me know the minute he found your note. I still wouldn't know if I hadn't decided to check on Sunbird. Sam seems to want to protect you from me, Susan. Isn't that interesting?"

His implication sparked Susan's own anger, but she bit her lip, reminding herself of her determination to stay in control. She did not, however, want the burden of her actions to fall on Sam's shoulders. She stood up and faced Kaleb squarely. "Sam had nothing to do with my decision to ride Moonflight and go to the village, Mr. Knight. I acted entirely on my own. I wasn't aware I was to check in with you every hour of the day and night."

His eyes gazed over her brief halter, burnished tan, and slim-fitting jeans. "I warned you about following paths you're not familiar with. I warned you about Moonflight and his unpredictable nature. You're lucky you've returned in one piece!"

"Moonflight was a perfect gentleman," Susan retorted with icy dignity. "Much more of a gentleman than his master. Besides, I've ridden to the village before, remember?" She took a deep breath. What was the point in going on? Kaleb Knight would always be the victor. The day had been much too beautiful and rewarding to let him ruin it.

Turning her back on him, she told Sam, "Luina had her baby today. It's a beautiful, healthy boy, and they named him after me."

Sam's face came alive with joy. He was obviously pleased on both counts.

"A boy named Sue?" Kaleb mocked sarcastically.

"No, a boy named Ray," came her flippant reply. "They took it from my last name, if it's any of your business. Now I'm going to call it a night. If you'll excuse me . . ."

Susan expected Kaleb to stop her, but he didn't, and she felt an inexplicable twinge of disappointment.

It was after nine o'clock when Susan woke the next morning, and even then it was a struggle to climb out of bed. She had worked on the painting of Luina and the baby until after midnight, and now the tree house reeked of paint and linseed oil. There wasn't a ripple of breeze to clear the air, she noticed, stepping out onto the veranda. The puffy white clouds overhead were the first she had seen since arriving on the island. There was an eerie stillness. Even the birds seemed to be chirping in whispers.

Sam's words came to mind. Sapphire Island didn't get many storms, he had said, but occasionally one would break open the sky. Laelia's husband had been killed during such a tempest.

Shaking off the unexpected shiver that traveled down her back, Susan went inside and made a pot of coffee, deciding to paint later on. There was something therapeutic about watching a subject come to life on her canvas. But last night, even though she'd worked diligently to capture Luina's beauty, her thoughts had remained fixed on Kaleb Knight.

Susan's reverie was interrupted by the telephone connecting to the main house.

"Mother and Aunt Essie are arriving around noon," came Kaleb's husky voice. "I suggest you meet me on the pier so we can give them a proper welcome."

"Like you were on the pier to welcome us?" Susan couldn't resist snapping back.

"You're a crusty little witch this morning, aren't you?" he drawled sarcastically.

"Only because you bring out the witch in me, Mr.

Knight. But don't worry. I'll be at the pier. After all, I can hardly hold your mother or aunt responsible for your foul disposition." She slammed the receiver down and clenched her fists. Why did he always provoke her so easily?

On the veranda sipping coffee she had plenty of time to relax—and too much time to think. Kaleb Knight loomed at every turn of thought. She had to admit it—she was miserable. Her feeling went beyond the sudden oppressive humidity that seemed to be weighing her down, or the lack of movement in the jungle. She felt a peculiar uneasiness.

The lagoon was as smooth as a glass plate. Was the ocean itself just as still? She closed her eyes and fought down a feeling of panic. The weather seemed unnatural, a reflection of her own morbid thoughts. At the heart of her dilemma stood Kaleb Knight. She loved him, and no matter what happened, her life would never be the same again.

Desperately needing Sam's friendly face to raise her spirits, Susan headed for the stables, and found him in Sunbird's stall.

"Sunbird is off her feed," he told her grimly. "It could mean her time is near or it could be the coming storm." The horse whinnied and tossed her head nervously.

Chilled to the core, Susan asked, "Then a storm *is* brewing! I thought the sky looked odd. Everything seems so still . . . so hushed. Will it be a bad one?"

Sam shrugged his massive shoulders. "There is no way to tell, Miss Susan, but if the wind begins soon—" He broke off, avoiding her concerned eyes. "I called Mr. Kaleb. He will come as soon as the seaplane lands."

"How long before the storm hits?" she asked, frightened at the thought of Helen and Essie flying in such weather.

"An hour, maybe two." He stroked Sunbird's quivering flanks and spoke to her in soft, soothing tones. "There is no way to tell. If we are lucky, it will not hit the island head-on."

"And if it does?" She held her breath.

Sam shrugged again, his brows furrowed. Susan longed to reach out and assure him, but only he knew the full savagery of a South Pacific storm.

"I'm supposed to meet Kaleb on the pier," she told him. "He wants me to be part of the welcoming committee."

Sam nodded. "Then go, Miss Susan, and tell Mr. Kaleb that everything is about the same here."

She hurried along the path, skirting the grass around the house, and then headed toward the beach. Kaleb was standing on the pier studying the sky. "It's about time," he muttered without looking at her.

"I don't see the plane," she returned with equal hostility. "Isn't that why I'm here, to meet the plane and give your mother and aunt what you call a proper welcome?"

Tension spun a web between them, yet when his green eyes finally flickered over her face, he smiled. "Yes, that's why you're here, though I'd like to think it's because you've stopped hating me."

"I think you've twisted your words around, Mr. Knight. I believe you're the one who has a monopoly in the hate department."

"Meaning?"

"Meaning you must hate me a great deal to work so hard at making my stay on the island miserable."

His voice was cool, his gaze steady. "If you're talking about the other night—"

"I'm talking about every night," she interrupted. "Every hour of every day and every night. You've subjected me to all sides of Kaleb Knight, and I've come away from each experience feeling ravaged of soul, mind, and body."

A brow hitched and white teeth flashed. "Believe me, love, you have not been ravaged, though the thought has often occurred to me. Just now, for example, I find myself wanting to sweep you away to some secluded cove and make love to you. Do you have any idea how fetching you look in that shocking pink getup? Your hair is a tumble, your cheeks aflame, and your eyes are shooting purple fire. I can see the pulse beating in your throat, my little pink sunbird, and it's warmly inviting. To place a kiss there would be ecstasy. To ravage your body would be both heaven and hell. I'm sorry for the things I said to you the other night, and I regret even more letting my desire overcome common decency. But I am, after all, a man, and every man has his weakness."

"And I'm supposed to forgive your weakness?" she asked, skirting around her true feelings. God help her if he discovered how much she loved him!

"That, my pink sunbird, is up to you."

"I am *not* your pink sunbird," she announced crisply, "though now isn't an appropriate time to discuss the matter. I have a message from Sam."

He shot her a look that made her bones melt, but then, just as suddenly, dimples creased his cheeks. "A message about Sunbird?" he asked. "Calling you a pink sunbird brought it to mind, did it? Did Sam tell you this was her first breeding? I thought we were in for a round of trouble at first. She was a bit skittish, totally overwhelmed by the great gray stallion. But she settled down soon enough, as soon as she realized what it was all about and that underneath Moonflight's tough exterior there beat the heart of a first-class lover. He swept her off her feet, in a manner of speaking, and she loved every minute of it."

His words carried a double meaning, and Susan fought for control. "Yes, it's about Sunbird," she replied coolly, ignoring the rest of his comment, though she seemed to be losing ground. He wore tight-fitting jeans and a pale-green body shirt that turned his skin to burnished teak and his eyes to glittering jade. "Sam said to tell you everything is about the same." She took a deep breath. "He also said it could be the coming storm that's making her jittery."

"The threat of a storm makes everyone jittery," Kaleb intoned, raising his eyes to the sky once again. The white clouds had massed together and were now tinged with gray. Swirls of gray, darkening before her eyes, lowered and gathered speed. She felt the first ripple of a breeze.

Kaleb cursed under his breath, his concern clearly directed toward the seaplane that was due any minute.

"S-Sam said the storm might not hit head-on," she said hesitantly.

"Sam was trying to reassure you, I suspect," Kaleb muttered. "He knows all the signs of a full-scale attack well enough. Damn! Where is that plane?"

The tone of his voice frightened Susan. "But would they take off from Pago Pago if a storm was on the way?" she asked.

"A storm is never actually on the way, Susan. It just seems to materialize out of nowhere. The flight from Pago Pago is barely twenty minutes. They probably figured they could outrace it." He looked at her then, and his eyes clouded with concern. "I want you to stay in the main house until it's all over. Agreed?"

Under normal circumstances she would have resented his condescending attitude, but now she took solace in the thought that he was trying to protect her. "I understand."

"Good! Then we should be perfectly in tune on one count."

They heard the engine before they saw the plane, and the look of relief on Kaleb's face was a beautiful sight to behold—almost as beautiful as the plane itself. As soon as the passengers arrived safely at the pier, the pilot took off again.

"We almost didn't get off the ground in Pago Pago," Helen sighed, giving Kaleb and Susan a hug. "If our island had been a few miles further—"

"We'd still be at the airport arguing," Essie intervened, distributing kisses liberally. "I swear, your mother can drive a hard bargain, dear nephew. She would have ended up piloting the plane herself if she and the pilot hadn't come to terms.

Helen looked down the length of her nose at Susan and lifted a brow at her son. "Well if you two don't beat all. Look at them, Essie Mae. Do you suppose they've eaten more than a mouthful since we left?"

"If that," Essie said, shaking her head. "Now what do you suppose they've been up to?"

"Well, we'll find out when we get to the house," Helen retorted with one eye on the sky. "I, for one, have no desire to be out in the open when the heavens open up!"

"Amen," Kaleb grunted, grabbing two suitcases.

Susan and Laelia carried the remaining bags, and headed for the house. By the time they reached the veranda, the trees had begun to sway.

"Secure the windows while I check on the tree house," Kaleb ordered, depositing the luggage in the entry. "We'll talk when I get back."

Following a frenzy of activity, the women regrouped in the garden room. "Where is that son of mine?" Helen interjected after several minutes.

Susan tried to smile. "Maybe he went to the stable to check on Sam and the horses. Sunbird's been off her feed."

"She's probably in labor," Helen sighed. "Lordy, wouldn't that be the final ticket?"

"A new foal as well as a new baby," Susan added. "Your sister gave birth to a beautiful son, Laelia." Susan had planned to let Kaleb make the announcement, but Laelia had looked so distressed—as she had every right to be considering her tragic experience during a similar storm—that Susan decided the girl needed some cheering up. The smile that spread across her face lightened Susan's heart.

Kaleb returned at that moment and the women converged on him with a barrage of questions about the baby.

"Whoa!" he cried. "All I know is that the baby was born and they named him Ray in honor of our beautiful guest, Miss McRay. She can probably tell you more since she was there and I wasn't."

All eyes turned to Susan, and she eagerly related her experience to them. Finally she broke off and bit her lip. "Will everything be okay at the village? I mean, can it weather the storm?"

Though Kaleb's green eyes were veiled, he nodded. "They've weathered many, though I've sent Sam along to help out. All hands are welcome at a time like this."

The thought of Sam riding all the way to the village in the ensuing storm turned Susan's blood cold, but she didn't comment. Why add to Laelia's uneasiness? The poor girl was in a state as it was.

Seeming to sense this perhaps more than anyone, Kaleb lightened his tone. "When the storm lifts, we'll ride to the village together, Laelia. I'd like to see the new addition as well as share a toast with the new father. In the meantime, I'll be with Sunbird."

CHAPTER
Nine

THAT EVENING, THE strong wind that had been blowing all afternoon swelled into a gale, but still the rain
didn't come.

"Maybe the storm's going to skirt around the island
after all," Susan reasoned, clasping her hands across
her chest to hug in her nervousness.

"Give me good old San Francisco fog," Essie responded with a mutter. She picked up a magazine and
tossed it down. "Storms give me the creeps, and I
don't care who knows it!"

"If it would just rain and push on," came Helen's
strained voice. "I've never known a storm to linger
this long."

Laelia had gone to the kitchen earlier, and now returned with a pot of tea and sandwiches. She looked pale.

Kaleb had been gone over six hours. Helen had tried to call the stable but received only static. Was he still there tending to Sunbird, or had he gone to the village in pursuit of Sam?

Susan walked over to the window and cringed at the sight outside. Palm trees were bent in two, and jungle vegetation flattened into a carpet. Usually, it was impossible to see the beach from the house, but now she caught glimpses of the sea through the cyclonic dance of the trees, and her breath caught in her throat. There was no beach! All-powerful, all-engulfing waves pummeled the shore. The beautiful beach Kaleb had shown her that first day had disappeared. She felt prickles of tears in back of her eyes and chided herself for being silly.

"There are tears in your eyes," Laelia said softly. "Are you concerned for Mr. Kaleb?"

Susan squeezed the girl's hand. "It's just the storm. I know Kaleb can take care of himself."

Laelia sighed deeply. "I thought that about my husband, Miss Susan, but he was crushed beneath a tree in a storm no worse than this. The rain has not come down yet. Why do you not carry sandwiches and coffee to the stable. At least you will put your mind at ease."

Susan had wanted to do just that for hours, but been afraid to ask. Now, with Laelia's vote of confidence, she faced Helen and Essie with determination. To her surprise, the two women agreed. Susan could report back if anything was amiss.

Laelia packed sandwiches into a waterproof pouch

and readied a thermos of black coffee while Susan promised to stay with Kaleb if the storm grew worse. As she headed out the door, it occurred to her that she might be safe from the elements, but she certainly wouldn't be safe from Kaleb Knight.

Halfway to the stable, lightning streaked the sky, followed by a roll of thunder that shook the ground. Twice Susan tripped over fallen trees and bushes. For every two footsteps forward, she took one back.

Suddenly, the rain came, pelting rain that soaked through her clothing so quickly that she gasped at the onslaught. Again lightning ripped the sky, closer this time, outlining the stable with an eerie light. Lunging the last few feet, she began pounding on the massive stable door, which was bolted shut against the storm. Thunder rumbled in response and she began to yell and kick at the door with a fury that matched the storm. "Damn you, Kaleb Knight!" she screamed over the din. "If you're not in there I'll—" Her shouted words became a shriek as hands reached out and jerked her off her feet.

"Shut up and stop acting like an idiot," Kaleb commanded. He carried her through a side door and set her down unceremoniously. "I never thought I'd see the day when a slip of a girl could raise more hackles than a storm!"

The scowl on his face appeared as ominous as the angry sky, and there was an electric moment of silence as his ruthless, gem-hard eyes traveled over her matted hair and wet jumpsuit, which clung to every curve. Little puddles gathered at her feet, and although she wasn't cold, she was shivering.

"You're a miserable looking mess, love. Suppose you tell me what you're doing here and just how you talked my mother into letting you out of the house. Or did you sneak out?"

At the sight of the man who, in the brief moments it had taken to drag her into the stable, had managed to get as wet as she, Susan's first instinct was to throw herself into his arms. But his heated words rekindled her anger. "I'm here because your family is worried sick, Kaleb Knight! When you discovered the lines were down, the least you could have done was return to the house long enough to report in!"

"I'm flattered by all the concern," Kaleb drawled sarcastically, "but it's really not that far from the house to the stable. Any one of you could've popped over to check up on me."

"My point exactly," Susan said coolly. "It's not that far. You could have 'popped' over to the house just as easily."

"I wasn't about to leave Sunbird. She's in foal and is having a tough time."

Kaleb's words were lost as thunder crashed overhead, but she had heard enough, and her anger dissolved into concern. Awkwardly, she held out the pouch of sandwiches and thermos of coffee. "Even midwives have to eat. Is there anything I can do?"

"Get out of those wet clothes, for one thing. You'll find some dry ones and a towel in the tack room. I think there's an extra cup, too, if you want some coffee. Just put the sandwiches on the desk. I'll take the time to eat later." He walked away.

Oh, why was he always so hateful? She knew there was a caring, sensitive side to him. She'd seen it more than once, but now his hostility seemed to be constant.

With a sigh, Susan headed for the tack room. Poor Sunbird. How terrible it would be if she lost her foal.

Don't think about it, she told herself. Everything would work out.

The clothes Kaleb had referred to consisted of a pair of white overalls at least six sizes too big, and Sam's blue jeans and a white T-shirt. She stripped, rubbing dry on a battered towel, and put on the overalls and T-shirt. After rolling up the pant legs three times, she decided she would be able to walk without tripping. Her shoes were soggy, but they would have to do.

She was working on her hair when Kaleb ambled in. He looked tired, but arrogant. "Why is her hair the first thing a woman thinks of?" he asked.

Susan shot him a look of pure hatred. "I suppose I should consider that a compliment, since you're referring to me as a woman instead of a child, but somehow, I think you're laughing between each word."

"I'm too tired to laugh, though I'll admit you do look like a child wearing your father's clothing. It beats catching pneumonia, though, don't you think?"

"Why aren't you taking care of Sunbird?" Susan echoed Kaleb's flippant tone. She laid the towel aside. Her hair, now a mass of tight ringlets, was hopeless.

"I came to get some of that coffee and a few minute's rest. Sunbird has herself in a lather and is getting nowhere. I had a mare like this once before. She was trying to birth two youngsters at the same time and neither would budge."

"Can Sunbird be having twins?"

"I don't think that's her problem. I think the foal is breech. I'll probably have to go in after it."

The thought terrified Susan, but she managed a

smile. "Whatever needs to be done, I'm sure you'll do it without difficulty."

"Of course I will, love." His jade eyes narrowed and his dimples flashed. "I always get what I go after."

"I assume you're talking about the women you want?" Susan asked casually, although when she poured coffee from the thermos her hands were shaking.

"Now why would you think that?" He grinned crookedly. "Could it be you have similar lustful urges on your mind?"

Their eyes met, and her heart beat wildly as his handsome face lowered, but the kiss, when it came, was brief and on her cheek.

"So much for my lust," he said perfunctorily. "Now finish your coffee like a good girl and let's see what we can do for Sunbird."

Unable to grasp what had just happened, only knowing she had been flatly rejected, Susan followed Kaleb to Sunbird's stall. She felt ill. In that brief moment before his lips had touched her cheek, she'd known complete surrender. If he had taken her in his arms, she wouldn't have resisted.

Inside the stall an overhead light illuminated the enclosure. As rain battered the roof and thunder rumbled, the light flickered off and on.

"If it goes, be prepared to grab the lantern on the stool," Kaleb instructed. "You'll have to hold it up and move it around as needed. Think you can handle that?"

Susan nodded, but her heart was thumping quickly. Sunbird was lathered from her strenuous efforts and groaning with pain. The sight of the mare tore at

Susan's heart. "Easy, girl," she whispered, dropping to her knees and stroking the mare's wet neck.

Kaleb left for a few moments, and returned stripped to the waist, carrying a steaming bucket of water. To this he added antiseptic which turned the water milky white. Susan tried to keep her eyes on the laboring mare, but the sight of Kaleb's bare chest and rippling muscles brought a breast-tingling lightness and a constriction of her throat.

"Keep talking to her," Kaleb said, apparently unaware of the effect he was having on her.

Sunbird was now taking short, rapid breaths. "Hang on, girl," Susan soothed, though she cast anxious eyes toward Kaleb.

Perspiration beaded across his forehead and brow, and he wiped it away with his arm. "Damn!" he swore, repositioning himself for a better angle. "Nothing but tail and rump, I'm afraid." He glanced at Susan in despair. "It's times like these when I wish I was a qualified vet. Foaling is never easy because of their long legs, but in a situation like this, I'd like better odds."

The light flickered again, and Kaleb shook his head. "Better move in closer with the lantern just in case."

"I helped with the birth of a calf one summer long ago," Susan said in a voice barely above a whisper, though she was now holding the lantern over Kaleb's shoulder. "They used a rope. Do you think that might help?"

Kaleb glanced at her briefly. "It might. With a slipknot, maybe I could draw out the hind legs. There's a rope on the wall in the tack room."

Susan ran to get it and returned to find Sunbird in

the middle of another quivering contraction.

"No time to lose," Kaleb muttered, quickly hitching a hind leg. "Okay," he finally gasped. "We're ready to go with the next contraction."

Susan held her breath as the mare began to quiver and then stiffen. With amazing strength, Kaleb pulled. Tiny hooves and then a soggy tail slipped out, and then with one final heave, the foal shot out into Kaleb's trembling arms.

Beside herself because the foal was already jerking and snorting, full of life, tears flooded Susan's cheeks.

"Damn! We did it!" Kaleb cheered with equal joy. "Will you just look at this little beauty?" He began to rub the pale-colored foal with a towel. "It's a filly and she's the color of a moonbeam."

"Little Moonbeam," Susan cooed, dropping to her knees. Soft brown eyes met hers and a wet nose nuzzled against her hand. "Oh, what a beautiful name!"

"Moonbeam it is, love," Kaleb grinned. "She's a sight to behold, isn't she?"

She was indeed. Sunbird rolled over then and struggled to her feet. She swung her head around to survey her offspring and, with a soft nicker, began to nudge the foal. Within minutes, the foal stood up on wobbly legs and nestled against the mare's side.

Kaleb stood wearily, stretching his back. "We won't be needed here any longer. Ready to share a sandwich?"

Suddenly ravenous, Susan nodded. "They make a beautiful sight," she said softly.

"And after the storm, you'll see delights you won't believe," Kaleb said huskily, helping her to her feet. "I can't explain it, it's just something you're going to have to see for yourself."

When their hands touched, the jolt of awareness between them was earth shattering, as acute as an exposed nerve. Struggling to control emotions running rampant, Susan could only nod.

While Kaleb showered in the bathroom connected to the tack room, Susan poured cups of coffee and set out cellophane-wrapped sandwiches.

"What did Laelia concoct this time," Kaleb asked, rejoining her.

"Sliced turkey." She handed him a sandwich. He'd buttoned his blue work shirt only halfway up, and her eyes became riveted to the glistening bronzed spot at the base of the V. His hair, still damp from his shower, curled up and over his ears.

"To us," he smiled, raising his cup in a toast. "To a job well done."

They touched cups and Susan flushed. The last time Kaleb had proposed a toast had been the night in the tree house when they had argued so terribly. She had been vulnerable to attack then, but was more vulnerable now. Was it the storm? The beautiful experience they had just shared? Her feelings for the man were approaching epidemic proportions.

They ate their sandwiches in silence, and although she couldn't meet his eyes, she could feel their molten probing. What was he thinking? How easy it would be to seduce her? Could he read her that easily? Oh, why couldn't she look at him with icy contempt, prove to him she wanted nothing to do with him as a man or as a friend? She had vowed he would never touch her again, yet she longed for the feel of his hands, the taste of his lips.

"It's one hell of a storm," Kaleb said, breaking into her thoughts. "It should have moved on by now."

She nodded and at last managed to meet his eyes. "Your mother mentioned that earlier."

"Hmmmm. The thunder seems to have moved off."

Susan hadn't noticed but now, with concentrated effort, she realized the thunder claps had grown faint. "Does that mean we can go back to the house now?"

"Not until the wind and rain stop as well. I'm afraid we're stuck here, love, and will be until *I* say it's safe to leave."

"You're not my keeper," Susan retorted. She felt panic consuming her. What if the storm lasted all night? She doubted she could survive another hour. "If I decide to leave, you can't stop me!"

Kaleb jumped off the desk and grabbed her arm. "The hell you say! I'm not about to chase all over the damned island looking for you!"

"I managed to get here on my own and I can get back on my own. Now let go of me." She wrenched free. "You're a . . . a . . . God, I don't know what you are!"

He smiled broadly, towering over her. "I'm a man who knows desire when I see it, Susan McRay, and the desire I see at the moment is in your eyes. Purple pools of desire. If I could, I'd turn back the clock to the day of your arrival. I wish you were just stepping off the seaplane, and I was there to greet you with open arms and a million promises. Promises to make your stay on the island one you would always remember. I wish we could start all over, my teinetiti. I'm afraid it would be the only way I could prove to you I'm not the scoundrel you seem to think I am."

"More words, Mr. Knight? Well, they are just words. I've listened to your honey-coated words before, and each time, you've pulled the rug out from under me. I won't let it happen again."

"And how do you propose to stop what's between us? Fate brought us together. Two floundering souls adrift with hearts turned to stone, but with a way to ease the pain, if you'd give it half a chance." He gripped her shoulders until they ached. "Can you deny the attraction between us?"

"Take your hands off me!" she cried, beating his chest with her fists. "Whatever attraction I felt for you disappeared days ago. Now I loathe you!"

"You want a fight, you little witch," Kaleb flung with a growl. "Well, you've got it!"

In a swoop, he lifted her into his arms, ignoring her flailing arms and legs and her cries of protest. From a great distance off, mingling with the blood rushing to her head, she could hear his angry mutterings. And then she was tossed into a darkened corner filled with sweet-smelling hay. She felt stifled as his weight landed on top of her. She cried out but was silenced by his brutal kiss. He had the strength of the world, and she was helpless.

"I feel passion coursing through your body," he said then, releasing her long enough to gaze down at her. "Tell me you hate me now. Look into my eyes and tell me how much you hate me. Deny what you're feeling, and I'll call you a liar!"

His arrogant words and invincible self-assurance renewed her own determination. As suddenly as he backed off to study her, she lurched away, scrambling to her feet and running to the door. Ignoring his shouts, she raced recklessly into the night. The gale-force wind and sheets of rain almost lifted her off her feet but she plunged on, stumbling in blinding anger and misery. Why had she allowed things to get so out of hand? She was a fool!

She heard Kaleb's voice behind her just as a large tree near the path crashed to the ground within inches of her. Before her shock could register, Kaleb pulled her back into the safety of his arms.

No words were spoken as he carried her back to the stable, but once inside, he set her down and kicked the door shut, giving it a final shove and bolting it against the storm. "Laelia's husband was killed by a falling tree," he muttered, facing her, "or didn't you hear about it. He was a seasoned warrior who had weathered many storms on Sapphire Island, but he wasn't spared death. The tree crushed his skull."

"Stop it!" Susan screamed. Even now she could be out on the pathway as dead as Laelia's husband. She began to shake, sweeping tremors convulsing her body.

They were both soaking wet. None too gently Kaleb shoved her toward the tack room. "We've got towels, but we're fresh out of clothes, though I suppose I could wear Sam's blue jeans." His green eyes held a flicker of amusement though his mouth remained firm. "What you do for clothing is your problem."

"My God, you can't be civil even when the situation is grim, can you?" Susan flung at him. "I appreciate your saving my life more than I can say, but that doesn't give you the right to treat me like a mangy dog that's gotten in your way. It would serve you right if I decided to shed my clothes and run around stark naked!"

"It probably would serve me," he replied wickedly,

"so you've got that much right anyway."

"You're hateful!" she shrieked. "Do you pride yourself on how cleverly you can turn my words around to suit your own purposes?"

"Maybe." His green eyes smoldered. "But I'm remembering a body quivering beneath my own and eyes glowing with purple fire. I'm remembering how close to heaven we were, and could be again."

He'd stepped closer, his hands skimming down her slim shoulders. There was no way to elude him; she didn't want to. Wild, primitive feelings were surging through her, and beneath his hands she trembled.

"I want you," he said simply as he worked the clasps on the overalls. "You're lovely and oh, so responsive. I need only touch you like this and this . . ."

The thickness of his voice embraced her senses, and she could scarcely breathe. He pulled down the straps and slipped the T-shirt over her head, and she stood naked before him. She was beyond caring. The gaze of his green eyes possessed her, devoured her beautifully shaped breasts now heaving outrageously. He reached out to one breast and then the other, causing her to arch her back and moan. Oh, but the feel of his hands was electrifying! Tiny waves of butterflies danced across her stomach and her knees grew weak, and when he reached down to kiss each pink-tipped mound, she thought she might faint from wanting him.

She watched fascinated as he stood back and slowly unbuttoned his shirt, and tossing it away, gathered her into his arms once again, pulling her close—oh, so close they were as one.

"The moon and the stars have never been as beautiful as you are at this moment," came his husky voice.

"I want to devour you. I want to make love to you until neither of us cares about tomorrow."

"Tomorrow will never come unless you love me now." Susan struggled, unable to catch her breath. Every nerve was caught up and they gently rocked together. Heat engulfed her like the sun on a summer afternoon. "Kiss me." She swayed. "Oh, God, kiss me!"

The last came as a plea, and when Kaleb's mouth sought hers, he found an open, sensually pliable mouth with enough passion to meet his own.

With animal grace, he lifted her up, cradling her in his arms, kissing her with passion gone primitive. For Susan, there would be no tomorrow if he didn't make love to her, and nothing beyond today if he did. She loved him, but he didn't love her in return. She knew it and had finally accepted it. Still, their lovemaking would be a piece of heaven, a moment of bliss.

Effortlessly, Kaleb carried her to the same hay-filled corner and lay her down gently, stretching out beside her. One leg covered hers as though to keep her from running away again. But running was no longer on her mind.

Hot kisses fanned her face as she moved against him, seeking fulfillment. His breath left her with a sigh as his mouth slipped to the base of her neck, and then down to her heaving breasts. Her hands, entwined in his hair, held him fast.

His magnificent body eased over hers as her limbs trembled with abandon. He had removed his wet jeans and she could feel every inch of his fiery skin.

"My God!" he groaned, drawing her even closer. There wasn't a part of her he didn't touch as he swept her along. She lifted her hands, clawing at the rippling muscles of his back. This was beauty complete. It was white fire, the roaring flames of passion between a man and a woman. She moved sensuously beneath him as her heart beat in great, unrelenting thumps. She wanted to cry out her love for him, but she held back that one final proof of all he meant to her. They would have only one moment of magic together.

As their passion stilled, she realized that once would never be enough. Kaleb's lips brushed the curve of her cheek. "You were wonderful," he whispered reaching down to kiss the tip of her nose. "It was magic."

"Hmmmm," she murmured, snuggling close, unwilling to give him up just yet, knowing that when she did it would be forever. "It's funny you should use that word. I was thinking the same thing."

"Then we're in sync, love, and it's about time. Listen. I think the rain has stopped."

"Hmmmm. I suppose we should be going." A blissful lethargy slid over her and her words drifted off. She didn't want to leave the warmth of his arms. She didn't want to face tommorrow ...

Susan woke up sometime during the night and realized Kaleb had wrapped a lightweight blanket around their naked bodies. He was asleep, his head turned toward her in peaceful innocence.

Thinking over what had happened between them pained her beyond tears. This night had become a brilliantly vibrant memory she would always cherish.

Kaleb stirred and stretched with a contented groan. When his eyes met hers, renewed passion glittered in them like emerald jewels. His hair was tousled, his chin rough with stubble, and his tanned body glistened. Her pulse quickened as a dimple creased his cheek. "You were sleeping so peacefully, I didn't have the heart to disturb you, love. I'm glad I didn't. It's wonderful to wake up beside the woman you've just made love to and find you desire her even more than before."

Susan shook her head and rolled away. "The magic of the moment, Kaleb, that's all it was. You said so yourself."

"And never to be repeated?" he asked. "Look at me, Susan. Look at me and tell me you don't want my hands on your body or my lips on yours like two lovers."

"But we aren't lovers," Susan insisted, struggling to sit up.

"We could be."

She had known from the beginning that any involvement with Kaleb Knight would be only temporary. "You're suggesting we have a two-week affair and then walk away from it, from each other, just like that!" She snapped her fingers.

"Oh, I don't know," he drawled, chewing on a slip of straw. "The airlines fly into San Francisco as well as Arizona. Maybe we could have a go at some long-term relationship. You know, no strings but certainly satisfying."

"Satisfying to you maybe, but hardly to me. Oh, Kaleb, don't you see? I shouldn't have let it go this far!"

"So why did you? Because you wanted me as badly as I wanted you. Come on, love, why do you keep denying it?"

"Because you're a male chauvinist and supremely

arrogant. I could probably forgive you for that, but I'll never forgive you for thinking of me as a conniving seductress who was working overtime to get Sam into bed."

"I was just jealous," he said in a comfortably lazy tone, rolling to a sitting position and gently drawing the straw he'd been chewing across her thigh. His green eyes danced. Was he teasing her again?

"Jealous? Men like you don't get jealous, Kaleb Knight. You think life is for the taking. Where and when is your only decision. I'm only sorry I'm so addlebrained I succumbed to your charms. You know the old saying, you'll be sorry in the morning. Well, I am, and I'll probably regret my indiscretion for many mornings to come."

"You really know how to flatter a guy, don't you," Kaleb grumbled though he didn't look perturbed.

"I'd like to go back to the house now," she said quickly. "My clothes should be dry by now."

"Dry enough to put on, if that's what you really want." He reached over and pulled the blanket away from her breasts. She gasped. "Was that a protest? Hmmmm, I wonder."

"Please," Susan begged, trying to move away from his outstretched hand. What was wrong with her? Could she find no way to resist him?

The morning light had grown brighter and now cast its glow across Kaleb's handsome face and desire-filled eyes. He stretched her out and lay down beside her, and then, like a moth drawn to a flame, her mouth opened to receive his hungry kiss.

"You're a witch!" Kaleb groaned, rolling on top of her, settling against her until her back dug into the straw. His hot kisses seared her throat and breasts.

"You've put a curse on me and I'll die if I can't have you."

"Kaleb, please don't," she cried softly, already weakening.

"Tell me you don't love what I'm doing to you," he whispered against her hair. "Tell me you're not longing for fulfillment. Tell me your back doesn't arch beneath me and your mouth doesn't open to me. Tell me to stop, my teinetiti, and I will. Tell me you really feel nothing, and I'll forget this night ever happened."

She couldn't. She was beyond words. She loved this man who taunted her with butterfly kisses and outrageous words, who could carry her to the height of ecstasy.

"Hmmmm, I thought so." He nuzzled her neck as he maneuvered an arm beneath her. "Neither of us can ignore it, so let's enjoy it, my sexy playmate, and we'll worry about tomorrow tomorrow."

Is that what she was to him, just a sexy playmate, Susan wondered as she pulled on her pink jumpsuit later that morning. Her hands shook as she tugged at the zipper. A sexy playmate to be used and then discarded.

Kaleb had pulled on Sam's blue jeans, and after giving her derrière a provocative squeeze, went to check on Sunbird and her foal.

Susan had considered slipping away while he was busy, but if what he'd said was true, the tree house might not be safe after the storm. Had nothing come away from the storm unscathed?

"You look a little rocky," Kaleb said, joining her in the tack room. He looked so concerned for a moment that her throat constricted. "The foal is suckling contentedly and Sunbird is well rested. Shall we go?"

He looked so alive—and totally male. In charge as he always would be. Nodding, she allowed him to take her arm as they walked out into a world washed clean. A balmy breeze blew in from the sea, and Susan's breath caught in her throat. Other than a few uprooted trees and scattered branches, along with a carpet of fallen leaves and flower petals, everything looked the same. Yet it was somehow different, too. The flowers seemed brighter, and the leaves sparkled like jewels. The sky overhead was incredibly cobalt, and before her eyes colonies of colorful birds swooped and chattered. "It's beautiful," she murmured. "I'm surprised more damage wasn't done."

"There's damage," he assured her. "You're just looking in the wrong places. You're seeing what you want to see—a damp, steaming jungle full of vibrant flowers. Even the birds look brighter."

"Your birds!" Susan exclaimed, stopping abruptly. "Are they all right?"

Kaleb grinned and whistled. Immediately, his pets swooped out of the trees.

"They never are very far away, are they?" She couldn't help smiling.

"It's my irresistible charm," he answered with a flash of white teeth. "They clamor to be near me and respond to my every call. Will you be as obedient?"

He was teasing her, but still her blood boiled. "I'm not one of your trained birds, Kaleb Knight. You can't whistle for me and expect me to respond!"

He stopped and pulled her close. "Maybe not, but will you be able to resist when I touch you like this, or this? Or kiss you like this?"

His mouth covered hers in a sensuous, delectable kiss until her feeble attempts to ward him off were abandoned.

"I thought not, love, and believe it or not, I find that thought very exciting. You smell like hay and horses and a night of love."

"And you, Kaleb Knight," she whispered fiercely, "had better face the fact that our night of love is over."

He looked down into her flushed face, his eyes very clear, very green. "We'll see, my teinetiti, we'll see. Perhaps our night of love is just beginning."

CHAPTER
Ten

WHEN THEY ARRIVED at the tree house, tears of relief filled Susan's eyes. Her little sanctuary, as she'd come to think of it, had withstood the storm. A few branches lay near the lagoon, and the veranda was strewn with leaves and petals, but the cottage had survived, intact.

Kaleb threw open the shutters to the morning sun and grinned. "When I build something, I build it to last." He broke off, eyeing her intently. "Do I detect a tear or two in your violet eyes?"

Susan nodded and quickly turned away. She felt like a fool. She loved the island, the tree house, and the man who reigned supreme. But soon she must leave them all.

"So you've become attached to the tree house, hmmmm?"

She nodded again, but couldn't speak. Not even when he put an arm around her and drew her close. "Sorry to frighten you, love. If it makes you feel better, I find your fondness for my little tree house quite touching. And as much as I'd like to stay around, I'd better check on Mother. I suggest you take two aspirin, a hot bath, and then come to the house for breakfast. Laelia's coffee and pineapple muffins have saved me more than once."

Susan watched Kaleb stroll out, but even after the door had closed behind him, she stood as though rooted to the spot, the feel of his arm still on her shoulder.

Finally she moved to the veranda and raised her face to the morning sun. The island had captured her in its magic spell, but all too soon she must leave it. Her heart would break unless she exorcised Kaleb Knight right now. She would never forget him, never stop loving him, but she must—she *must*—stay away from him.

An hour later Susan joined her hostesses and Kaleb on the veranda. Although she kept her eyes turned away from him, she noticed that he had changed into white slacks and a shirt.

"Ah, now our morning is complete." Helen smiled, giving Susan a hug. "Are you hungry? Laelia has whipped up a celebration breakfast of sorts."

"I must say, you do look fetching and no worse for wear after your ordeal in the stable," Essie remarked, kissing Susan's cheek.

Her breath stopped. She was forced to meet Kaleb's amused expression. "Ordeal?" she asked.

"Why, the foaling, of course. We understand it was your idea to use a rope."

Kaleb's eyes glinted wickedly. "Susan had a number of ideas actually. She might be a little slip of a gal and appear too beautiful to have brains, but let me tell you, she's full of surprises."

Susan found it difficult to acknowledge Kaleb's presence let alone respond to his comment. He was behaving abominably—as she should have expected.

"Come have some coffee," he drawled. "Nothing tastes as good as that first cup in the morning."

She took the cup and turned her back to him. "Has anyone heard from Sam?" she asked, hoping a change of subject would calm her shaking hands.

Helen nodded. "He checked in a few minutes ago, I'm happy to say. There was only minor damage to the village, nothing the people can't handle. He was delighted to hear about the filly. Kaleb was just telling us it was your idea to name her Moonbeam."

"Kaleb also mentioned your sketches," Helen went on. "We'd love to see them. He tells us Sam drew a sketch of you. You know, it's the first I've heard of his artistic talents."

"My sketches are actually just forerunners to my paintings," Susan said, trying to keep her voice even. "And Sam does have talent. I've offered to give him some lessons."

Helen shook her head. "Well, you certainly can't tell a book by its cover, can you?"

"No, you certainly can't," Kaleb smiled wryly. "Books have many pages too."

Everything he said held a double meaning, and Susan was furious. Double damn him and his blatant nerve! Why couldn't he leave her alone?

Laelia chose that moment to serve breakfast—pineapple muffins, sausage, scrambled eggs, and fresh orange juice, all of which were excellent.

Halfway through the meal, Essie poked Helen's arm. "They're actually eating like they're hungry, dear Helen. We never did find out what caused them to go off their feed while we were gone."

"Nor do I think they want to tell us, Essie Mae, so I think we should drop the subject."

"Come now," Kaleb said easily. "You're reading too much into it. Susan has been knee-deep in art and I've been knee-deep in my book. We've been two artists at work with little thought of food, right Susan?"

Helen lifted a suspicious brow. "You don't say. Well, far be it from me to interfere with creative impulses. Anyway, the morning is much too beautiful to spend taxing this old brain. Smell the air. Isn't it refreshing?"

"The air smells terrific in San Francisco, too, dear Helen," Essie remarked heatedly.

Susan moved to the railing to escape their argument. The air was wonderfully refreshing, but for the moment the scents floating in on the breeze were blanketed because Kaleb had moved to her side. His nearness was stifling, though she managed to whisper, "Why did you cover up for their benefit?"

"I thought you needed rescuing," he answered evenly. "Mother would have asked endless questions and you would have ended up embarrassed. Besides, we need some sort of a cover if we're going to continue romping about in the hay. Unless you want to tell them what we've been up to."

She was furious. "How dare you! The only embarrassment I'm likely to suffer is because of my association with you! Your arrogance is unbelievable.

What happened between us is over. Over!"

"Hush, my serpent-tongued vixen. They're going to stop arguing long enough to realize we're arguing too, which in turn will give them their first hint that not all is well in paradise. Why burst their bubble? The least we can do is smile at one another and make their romantic hearts happy."

"Never!" Susan hissed through clenched teeth. "You won't play games with me!"

"Games?" he queried. "I'd rather think of it as a pagan love ritual, a mild one at that. Did you know there's a tribe of natives in the New Hebrides Islands who demand that their women have two front teeth knocked out with a rock so they can be proclaimed as trustworthy, true, and affectionately forever a woman possessed?"

"My God!" Susan groaned, her stomach churning. "Are you proposing I give up my two front teeth because in a moment of madness I allowed you to make love to me?"

Kaleb merely grinned. "Relax, love. I'm not proposing anything."

"Then I'm upset over nothing, is what you're saying?"

"Keep guessing," he said huskily. "You're getting warmer."

"Damn it, Kaleb, stop talking in circles! You're insane."

His green eyes darkened and he leaned over and kissed the tip of her nose. "Perhaps, but then life is insane. By the way, I've never seen you look more ravishing." A dimple creased his cheek. "Scrubbed your face clean so I'd get a glimpse of the real you and hopefully get turned off, eh?"

His perception was incredible. "Yes, as a matter of fact," she admitted.

"Well, you've defeated your purpose, love. What I see is a lovely, desirable woman. Freckles may dance across your nose and flushed cheeks, but your eyes have chips of purple fire in them. I read you well, my teinetiti."

He was unbearably close, barely a breath away, his face carved of teak and stone. Only his eyes seemed alive, and they were the color of the jungle and as threatening as the recent storm. She looked into them for one brief, drowning moment, fighting the tremors racing through her before she stood tall and raised her chin.

"If you can read me so well, then you must know how much I regret my moment of madness. I'll admit there is something between us . . . a physical attraction, I suppose you would have to call it. But that's all. Now if you'll excuse me, I'm going to spend the day painting to soothe my frazzled nerves. You really do bring out the worst in me, Kaleb Knight."

"Only because you bring out the lust in me, my teinetiti. But don't worry. I'll be with Laelia at the village, so you'll be safe for a few hours."

"Safe? I'd prefer to think of it as being at peace." Suppressing the urge to continue their pointless bickering until Kaleb gave in, she returned to the older women. Their expressions told her they had overheard at least part of the conversation.

"Is there a problem, dear?" Helen asked carefully.

"Looks like that son of yours has been causing trouble," Essie grumbled.

Kaleb sauntered up behind Susan and placed a possessive arm around her waist. "I'm innocent," he said, displaying a fetching smile. "On the contrary, Susan and I have been getting on famously, though I do think she's rather done in after last night's excitement. Perhaps you should take a nap, love. We didn't get much sleep."

"Perhaps you're right, love," Susan interrupted with mock sweetness. "Though I'd rather paint away my blahs than waste time sleeping. Oh, by the way, if you should happen to see Sam, tell him to drop by the tree house when he can find the time. I'd like to begin working with him."

"So that's how the land lies," Kaleb whispered in her ear. Aloud he said, "I'll tell him, love. Just don't hold your breath. His duties are many and varied."

"Twenty-four hours a day?" Susan asked, lifting a brow, pleased with her comeback.

"Of course not twenty-four hours a day," Helen grumbled. "Where are your manners, Kaleb? You sound as though you resent Susan's wanting to teach Sam how to paint. Personally, I think it's an outstanding idea."

Susan removed herself from Kaleb's grasp. "Thank you," she said sweetly. "Now I really should get to work. Thank Laelia for the wonderful breakfast. I enjoyed it." She headed back to the tree house.

Moments later, Kaleb caught up with her on the path. "What the hell are you trying to pull?" he demanded. "For a woman who claims to hate men, you're doing a fine job of collecting them."

They were standing amid a tangle of creeping vanilla vines laced with white orchids, and Susan reached up and plucked one of the prettiest. "You're talking in circles again," she said, waving the orchid under his nose. She willed her heart to stop pounding and her legs to stay firm. She'd gone through so many emotional peaks and valleys with this maddeningly complex man, she realized now—almost too late—that to survive she must fight him with his own tools of aggravation and arrogance.

"You're accusing me of collecting men because I allowed you to make love to me...and because I want to give Sam a few lessons in oil painting? How droll. And by the way, I never professed to hate men. I think you've managed to twist your own feelings to serve your own purposes. You know what they say, misery loves company."

His jade eyes narrowed. "Are you calling me a woman hater?"

"Well, aren't you?"

"Have I acted like one?"

"You're acting like one now," she flung back, narrowing her own eyes in contempt. "You're not my keeper, yet you continue to act like one. I'm supposed to jump through your primitive chauvinistic hoop, and when I don't I receive twenty lashes of your forked tongue. You have the nerve to tell me you don't play games, yet you've been playing one very intense game of cat and mouse since the first moment we met. Enough is enough. I'm going to the tree house to paint. I'll teach Sam the finer points of art, if he's agreeable, and I'll ride Moonflight when and where I want to. If I choose, I'll run into the jungle and face that bloody red-eyed boar, but the choice will be mine. I have two weeks left and you won't ruin them for me. We'll either become friendly enemies—at the very best—or we'll ignore each other completely. You do your thing and I'll do mine."

Her cheeks were flushed when her eyes met his,

but instead of the anger she'd expected to see, his eyes flickered with amusement. "We're lovers on an island paradise," he spoke huskily. "We were given the pleasure of an unforgettable night and now we must endure an intolerable day. Why, Susan? Must you fight your feelings with such force that you blind yourself to the truth? I can see it in your eyes right now. You want me as much as I want you. What we have between us is as powerful as the storm that's just passed, but I won't force myself on you. Neither can I promise to stay away from you. Fate, like the storm, will uncover the stones, and we'll just wait and see what we find."

His final words were almost whispered, and then he was gone, his long strides muffled against the carpet of leaves.

By midday, Susan had nearly completed the portrait of Luina and the baby. She was using a quick-drying matte medium with the oils, and hoped that whatever work she managed to complete now would soon be dry enough to handle. The portrait was good, probably the best work she had ever done. It seemed strange that she had been able to find such inspiration amid her turbulent feelings and sadness. Or maybe it had been because of them.

Taking a few minutes to relax and study her efforts with a glass of iced tea, she almost missed the light rap at the door. Hurrying, praying it was Sam—anyone but Kaleb—she greeted the tall Samoan with open arms. It was the first time she had seen him since the storm, and he was a sight for weary eyes!

"Have I come at a bad time?" he asked, giving her a lopsided grin.

"You could never come at a bad time," she assured him, pulling him into the living room. He wore blue jeans and a cotton shirt, and though she found herself wondering briefly if they were the blue jeans Kaleb had donned during the storm, she immediately pushed such a disturbing thought aside. "Iced tea?" she asked, heading for the kitchen.

Sam nodded, eyeing her sloppy, paint-spattered pants and shirt.

"I've never mastered the art of artwork without making a mess," she laughed, handing him a tall glass. "Come see what I've done."

Sam was impressed. "You are very good, Miss Susan," he said admiringly. "Will it be difficult for me to learn all the different colors?"

"As simple as riding Moonflight," she teased. "What would you like to do first? Anything you choose would be appropriate after you've learned to mix colors and handle a brush."

Sam chose the lagoon, and Susan was delighted. For several hours they worked without interruption. Sam's feeling for color was incredible, and his sense of touch pure magic.

It was after five o'clock when Susan left him trying to capture a difficult palm tree and went into the living room to call Helen. "Sam and I are still knee-deep in paint," she told her, "so I thought I'd just whip up a bite to eat here. He really is a natural, though I might be creating a monster. Don't be surprised if he suddenly decides he'd rather paint than work."

Helen laughed. "I'm not worried, dear. You just tell Sam to enjoy his new venture, you hear?"

Warmed by Helen's words, Susan prepared dinner and went to fetch Sam, who had finished the palm tree and was working on the sand.

"It looks like something right out of fantasyland it's so pink," she told him, "but you've captured the colors to perfection."

"White, flesh, and a touch of burnt sienna." Sam grinned triumphantly.

Nodding, Susan removed the brush from his hand. "Even Picasso had to eat. This has been the one bright spot of my trip—well, almost. It would be difficult to top the birth of Luina's baby and the foal."

"You are our star shining bright, Miss Susan," Sam said softly. "Everyone thinks of you as one with us."

They were seated at the table and Susan dished up Sam's plate. "Because I helped deliver Luina's baby?" she asked, gulping back her emotions. "I did what had to be done, Sam."

"But it is more than that, Miss Susan." He stopped and flushed. "But it is not for me to say. In a few days, we will have our ceremony at the water. We will fish on the reef by torchlight. Luina said you would like to join us, and we would be honored."

"It would be an honor for *me!*" Susan exclaimed. "It sounds so exciting. Will Mr. Knight attend?"

Sam's white teeth gleamed. "Yes, Miss Susan. It is one of his favorite of our island festivities, but don't worry. All will go well."

"So you've caught wind of the fact all is not well between us?"

"Everyone knows, Miss Susan. Our island has ways of knowing things others do not. You love him and he is fighting his love for you."

Susan watched Sam hoist a forkful to his mouth and her heart stopped. "You're mistaken," she said, barely above a whisper. "Mr. Knight doesn't love me.

He's incapable of love. I won't deny how I feel, but it's a lost cause."

"He has turned his love into hostility because he is frightened, Miss Susan. He was hurt badly and he is afraid."

"I was hurt, too, Sam, but my heart hasn't frozen over into a lump of stone because of it."

"Different people respond in different ways," he said. "And he is a man different than most. He will not be able to fight it forever."

"But I don't have forever, Sam. I'm leaving in two weeks."

He shrugged. "Two weeks can be a lifetime. When I left the stable, he was there with Sunbird and her foal. I know his eyes. When they are the color of wild cane, he is unhappy. I think he is unhappy because he has made you unhappy. Is that not the sign of love?"

Susan appreciated what Sam was trying to do, but it wouldn't work. Although Sam knew Kaleb well, she doubted that anyone completely knew the man who would be king.

CHAPTER
Eleven

THE BREEZE WAS bewitching and the sun cast golden ripples across the lagoon. Susan lay at ease on the shimmering pink sand and watched the sight unfolding before her.

It had been four days since she had seen Kaleb, four days since the lesson with Sam, and although she'd kept busy painting, visiting Sunbird and her little foal, and even hiking the upper cliffs (with Sam's help) to get her first glimpse of the nesting place of the torquoisine parrakeets, her heart was still tortured.

She had taken her meals at the house, under Helen and Essie's watchful eye, and although Helen had attempted to make excuses for her absent son, Susan's emotions played havoc with every part of her body.

She knew what it was like to become wrapped up in work, but was that the real reason he had stayed out of sight?

Susan rolled over onto her stomach and sighed. She should be elated with the turn of events, yet all she felt was sad emptiness. She missed his handsome, craggy face and teasing emerald eyes. She missed his bold arrogance. She missed the way he could drive her to instant fury and then wicked desire. He was the most maddening man she had ever met, and he would be the most difficult to forget.

The soft breeze blowing across the lagoon couldn't cool her cheeks. Tonight, she would ride to the village with Laelia and Sam and join the torchlight festivities. Tomorrow would be the feast, the fia fia. Kaleb was supposed to attend, but would he?

"It seems a long time ago I told you to watch out for the rays of our Samoan sun," Laelia said pertly, dropping to her knees beside Susan. "And now look at you. You are one with the island . . . as brown as a coconut. I bring a message from Miss Helen. Dinner will be served at four o'clock, and then we will ride."

"I've been on the beach since sunup, Laelia. I needed some time to think. Are you looking forward to tonight?"

"Oh, yes!" the girl exclaimed. "It is a special time. We have many things to celebrate. Wear your swimming suit beneath your clothing, and then you can join us on the reef."

"Whoa!" Susan laughed. "I'm just going along to watch."

"But everyone will fish," Laelia protested. "The more fish we catch, the more fish we will have to eat tomorrow."

Susan shook her head. "Well, I'm game, but I'd better warn you. I can't catch a trout with a Garcia Special let alone a spear."

"A Garcia Special?"

"It's a kind of fishing reel. It's supposed to put the odds in the fisherman's favor, but the fish seem to think it's the other way around. Put a spear in my hand by torchlight and I'll probably skewer my toe."

"But we will teach you," Laelia insisted. "You will be surprised how easy it is."

Susan looked at the beautiful girl who had become her good friend. "And does Mr. Knight join in and fish with the villagers?"

"Yes, he does," Laelia said, lowering her eyes. "But this time . . . Well, we will have to wait and see."

"Then you think he will stay away because of me?"

"Mr. Kaleb is fighting with a part of himself, Miss Susan. He buries himself in his work, and this he has done before, but now, he buries his feelings as well. Miss Helen and Miss Essie are concerned. He eats very little and grumbles much."

"And if he doesn't go tonight, I'll be to blame," Susan flung, poking her toe in the sand. "Damn it, Laelia, why does everything have to be so complicated? I don't want to keep him away from his friends and the things he loves. I'll stay here and he can go. It's his place to be there for the festivities, not mine."

Laelia shook her head. "He is a stubborn man. If he has decided not to go, it won't matter if you stay behind. He will refuse either way. He is in love with you and hates himself for his weakness. He did not want to love again, Miss Susan, but he will know the truth soon."

"You should join forces with Sam," Susan said

dejectedly. "You both think Mr. Knight is in love with me, and you're both terribly wrong. He's attracted to me and he's a man. Maybe Samoan men are different and that's what's led you astray."

"Men are men all over the world," Laelia said softly, "and love is the same. Love is never easy."

They saddled up shortly before six o'clock just as the sky was showing the first traces of night. Dinner had been a hurried affair of shrimp salad and crusty rolls, and by the time coffee was served, it looked as though Kaleb had decided to stay behind. No one was more surprised than Susan when he appeared at the stable at the last minute.

Now, with Sam in the lead on a black gelding followed by Laelia on the dappled mare, Susan sat square in the saddle on Moonflight while her heart thumped a crazy tune in her chest. Kaleb rode the red stallion, bringing up the rear.

They all wore jeans and western-style shirts, and it seemed strange to be dressed in western apparel riding horseback along a Samoan beach.

With a dig of her heels, Susan urged the big stallion on until she was abreast of Sam and Laelia. She didn't want to stay behind with Kaleb, whose green eyes held a strange look. "How will we find our way back in the dead of night?" she asked of Sam.

"With a cloth over their eyes the horses could find their way home," he replied.

They had come to a narrow spot near the river and had to trot single file. Once again Susan was at the rear with Kaleb.

"Are you trying to avoid me?" he asked sarcastically.

"No more than you've tried to avoid me all week," she flung back at him.

"You think that, do you? Why don't you believe I was so involved in my book that I couldn't set it aside? When the words come, I have to drop everything else. I thought you, more than anyone, would understand that."

Susan chanced a quick glance at his profile. Was he serious? Had she, along with everyone else, made too much of his four-day hibernation? "I thought you had made your choice."

Kaleb raised his brows in mocking amusement. "What choice is that, love?"

"I presented the only alternatives," she told him. "We either become friendly enemies or ignore each other completely."

"And you assumed I'd decided on the latter. That's interesting. My choice was obviously important to you."

His words brought her blood to simmer. "Don't flatter yourself," she said sharply. "If you must know, the last four days have been delightfully peaceful. I managed to complete my paintings and still find time to loll in the sun. I've hardly been pining away over the loss of the devil himself!"

"I'm glad." A note of irony rang in his voice. "I wouldn't be interested in you if you were a moaning female."

She sat straighter in the saddle and lifted her chin. "So why are you interested in me?" she asked. She could have ended the conversation easily by simply riding ahead. Why did she remain beside him, goading him into answers she didn't want to hear?

"Let's just say I have a barbaric attraction for wild

fillies and an uncontrollable urge to tame them." His
eyes glinted in the evening shadows, raking over her
legs incased in slim jeans and her full breasts beneath
a yellow shirt. His eyes then drifted to her tumble of
hair and flushed cheeks. "Let's say if I wanted to stay
away from you I couldn't. I still think we would make
outrageous lovers."

He had caught her off guard again. She felt trapped,
vulnerable.

"Relax," he said suddenly. "I'm not going to rape
you on horseback, so enjoy the ride. Look at the
flowers."

Wild, exotic flowers were draped like a colorful
umbrella overhead, tumbling down branches, and
covering the ground in a profusion of color, but Susan's thoughts were focused on the man who rode
beside her. Her love for him was flaming out of control. Did he know it? Would he take advantage of her?

Kaleb's voice was husky when he spoke. "Beautiful Susan. Worldly yet innocent. I wonder if you
know what you do to me."

She knew what he did to her and that was the hell
of it. Without responding, she urged Moonflight into
a gallop, trying to outrace her thundering heart.

When they arrived at the village, there was the
usual greeting of laughing children and barking dogs.
The air seemed to be filled with love and well-being.
Bright torches turned the scent into a land of enchantment.

An underground oven was steaming in readiness
for tomorrow's feast, and although the villagers wore
an array of attire from baggy trousers to muumuu-
style dresses, everyone wore flowered leis around
their necks and ankles. The women wore flowers in

their hair as well, and children carried baskets heaped with orchids, Gardenia, frangipani, and Hibiscus.

Dismounting and handing the reins to Sam, Susan and Laelia were greeted with open arms. Luina and Nuta placed white orchid leis around their necks while Chief Fua gave them his blessing. Everyone toasted their survival of the storm, their new friend Susan, Luina and the new baby, and life's plentiful bounty. More torches were lit, songs were sung and dances performed. Susan found herself trembling, unbelievably moved.

"You're quivering like a leaf in a windstorm," Kaleb whispered in her ear. "Is it because of the excitement or are you ill?"

He had removed his shirt and stood bare-chested beside her. A lei of creamy white Plumaria encircled his neck, its heady scent mingling with the smell of his soap and after shave. "I'm drunk on the excitement of it all," she admitted. "I've never seen anything so beautiful. Look at their faces. How wonderful it would be to feel that free, that happy."

"I'm looking at the most breathtaking face of all, my teinetiti. If I could capture your expression in a book, it would sell a million copies."

"You're caught up in the moment, too," she told him with a constriction of her throat. "It's infectious."

"I'm caught up by the nearness of you."

Their eyes met and by torchlight she could see the burning desire in his eyes. Yet he made no move to touch her. He was in control. It was she who ached for the feel of his arms, the taste of his lips. "But you're not touching me."

"Do you want me to touch you?" he asked. His eyes had become dark, passionate pools. "Love is free and uncomplicated in Samoa. No one would mind if I kissed you or took you off into the jungle. Is that what you want? Tell me what you want, my teinetiti."

What she wanted was his love. Not just another night of passion. Yet her desire for him was somehow canceling out her thoughts and promises to stay away from him.

He had maneuvered her into the shadows, and when his lips brushed her cheek, her blood turned to liquid fire. His hands slipped around her waist and then upwards, molding her firm breasts. "I want to make love to you," he whispered huskily, pressing her back against a tree. "I want to kiss your breasts and all the other places that are screaming for my touch."

She wanted nothing more than to reach up and take his face into her hands, to lose herself amid the fires raging free. But how could she? How could she give in to another night of love knowing that when it was over her heart would be empty? "Please!" she cried, trying to twist away. "Don't!"

"Don't what, my teinetiti? Don't touch you like this? Everything about you is crying for love. Why fight it? I had a taste of heaven wrapped in your arms, and I know you felt it, too. Why deny what our bodies clamor for? You're trembling but not only because of the enchantment around us. You want me as much as I want you."

Slowly, deliberately, he undid the buttons on her shirt. Beneath, covered by a tiny bit of material, her breasts rose and fell in rhythm. It couldn't be happening again, yet it was!

"You're wearing a swimsuit so no one will think twice if I remove your shirt." His voice was thick, almost slurred as he dropped her shirt to the ground. Slowly, sensually, his hands wound around to her back and then down to her firm bottom. He pulled her close until the buckle of his belt pressed against her stomach.

Susan's face lifted of its own accord to meet his urgent kiss. She moaned, a sound from the depths of her throat, as his warm tongue probed deeply, seeking all the pleasures there were to know. She clung to him, pressing her body against his sinewy muscles, her hands digging into the flesh of his back.

"Your body drives me wild," he groaned, lifting her off the ground, her breasts pressed against his chest. "I can feel your heart pounding, taste your sweet breath. There is no end to the fires you ignite in me and only one way to extinguish them. I want to make love to you as no man has ever made love before. Every hour of every day. I ache for the feel of your body under mine."

"We can't!" Susan gasped as though her next breath might be her last. "We have to join the others." She twisted, desperately trying to break loose. She wanted Kaleb, body and soul, but it was wrong. Oh, God, it was wrong!

Kaleb released her, inch by inch, until she slid down the length of him. She felt as though she'd been plugged into an electrical outlet with every nerve ending aflame. One more moment and it would be too late. One more moment and she would forget he was the man who didn't love her.

Kaleb sighed. "Yes, I suppose we should join the others. I wouldn't want you to miss any of the celebration. We have the rest of the night, after all. We'll save this for later."

Never! she cried silently. She had escaped this time, and wouldn't get herself in such a situation ever again.

Minutes later she sat on the sand watching the torchlights flicker in the breeze. The entire village had joined in the spear fishing, young and old alike. Although they had prodded her to try her hand at their marvelous sport, she had declined, content to sit on the beach and watch. She desperately needed this time to sort out her confused thoughts.

Luina sat beside her with the baby at her breast. With the exception of one very old lady and Mutu, who'd also stayed behind, she seemed to be the only villager who wasn't in the water.

"It looks like the night has a thousand eyes," Luina said, referring to the weaving torches. "Last time Tuai speared the most fish. You should be out there with them, Miss Susan. It is fun and easy."

"I don't mind watching," Susan replied. "It's a beautiful sight from here."

"When Tuai . . . Well, before we became husband and wife, I would sometimes sit on the sand and watch the flickering torchlights and wonder which was held by my man's hand. Do you not wonder which one is held by Kaleb?"

"Mr. Kaleb is not my man," Susan said stiffly.

"Ah, but he should be. Do you not love him?"

"My love for him is not enough."

"Love is always enough, Miss Susan. I can see the way he looks at you. I can see the love in your eyes."

A lump formed in Susan's throat, causing tears to well and spill. "That's just it. You can see the love in my eyes," she retorted, "but Kaleb doesn't feel it. His needs are different than mine."

"Are you so certain?" Luina asked. "Has he not fooled himself with one kind of affection when he actually feels another? Are you not asking too much of him? He is a man who has had his heart broken. He needs time for it to heal. Will you not give him that time if you love him?"

Susan's pulse raced. Was the whole world against her? "It's the other way around! He's asking too much of me!" She was sorry the moment the words were out of her mouth. It wasn't Luina's fault Kaleb was the devil and she was a fool. "I-I'm sorry," she said, reaching for the girl's hand. "I wanted this night to be special, and now all I foresee is heartache and pain."

She broke off, chewing her lip. When Kaleb came out of the water, what would happen? The fishing would end and he would expect to pick up where they had left off. He would expect her to fall into his arms in wild abandon, and nothing she could say or do would convince him she wanted no part of his night of love.

Worse yet, she knew how she would react when he came out of the water and touched her. She knew how she'd felt when he'd stripped off his pants before going into the water. By torchlight, and in the briefest of swim trunks, his body had glistened in the flickering light.

But, if she wasn't around when the time came ... "I'm going back to the village to wait," Susan said suddenly, praying Luina didn't see through her scheme. "Mutu is still there and I'll visit with him."

Susan couldn't see Luina's face, but she knew the girl was surprised. Well, so be it. Susan was fighting for her life.

Her plan was to return to the village, mount Moon-flight, and then ride like the wind. Sam had brought along a flashlight. She would take it from his saddle-bag, and with his words giving her courage—"With a cloth over their eyes the horses could find their way home"—she would return to the tree house.

The trouble began when she missed the trail. It wasn't far from the reef to the village, only a half mile or so, and on a direct line. But she'd followed the procession to the reef by torchlight and in the company of the villagers, who knew where they were going. Now, by the light of only a half moon, she not only lost the trail but didn't have the foggiest notion of how to return to the beach. Was she wandering around in circles?

Now what, she wondered, leaning against a tree. The sounds of the villagers' happy cheers and laughter had faded away, replaced by night sounds of the jungle, whisperings rising to a crescendo. Unseen creatures skittered among the trees and night birds flapped their wings in flight. It looked as though Kaleb would have the last laugh after all. He had warned her long ago about the dangers of getting lost in the jungle.

With a sigh, Susan trudged on, tripping over creeping vines with every step. Something slithered beside her leg and she stifled a cry. It would be better not to call out for help. She might be near the village, maybe on the very outskirts, and Mutu would hear. But she might also be too far away for anyone to hear her. Her breath would be wasted then, and she needed every breath to keep control.

She pictured the island in her mind. Surely she would come to either the reef or the river sooner or later. She wouldn't let herself think about the center of the island, that vast area Kaleb had warned her about, wild and treacherous with rampaging boar and snares. She would have to cross the river to reach that part of the island, wouldn't she? Or would she? Right now she couldn't be certain of anything.

Walking was tedious at best. In some places, the tangled vines and brush were totally impenetrable, and she had to seek another direction. There was no way she could tell where these detours were leading her, or how long she had been floundering about. She became bogged down in several marshy spots that had occurred after the rain, but it wasn't until the moon and twinkling stars had disappeared, hidden by a vast blanket of entwined trees, that she realized she had reached the deep recesses of the island. Somehow she had bypassed the river.

Weary and aching in every bone, she knew she couldn't go on. She would have to wait out the night and hope that by the light of early dawn she could find her way out. Had Kaleb discovered her absence? Had he alerted the village? Were they looking for her even now, perhaps within calling distance? She opened her mouth, but no sound came out.

She found a perch in a nearby tree, a sturdy tangle of branches that would hold her weary body. Utterly exhausted, she was finally able to sleep.

CHAPTER
Twelve

SUSAN WAS AWAKENED early the next morning by the rustle of leaves very close to her head. Without thinking, she gasped and rolled from the branch, swinging to the ground. Only then, safe on terra firma, did she allow herself to seek out what had awakened her. There on the branch where she had spent the night slithered a green-tinged snake. Her eyes remained riveted as it entwined its body around and around, its beady black eyes watchful while its tongue darted in and out.

Shaking and feeling sick to her stomach, Susan moved across the small clearing and sat down on a log. Holding her body close, she buried her head on her knees. She had survived the night—there was little point in dwelling on what might have slithered across her body while she slept. But would she survive the new day?

Bird songs pierced the morning stillness. Lilting, beautiful, they revived her for the trek ahead. She mustn't sit still and wait for someone to find her. She could die of hunger and rot away before help came. She must press on through the velvety green gloom.

She appeared to be in some sort of a rain forest, where even the flowers grew to gigantic proportions. Orchids ranging from dark lavender to mossy green dripped from every tree, and in places massive tree ferns grew upwards of thirty feet, forming a green canopy that blotted out the sky. She came across a glade of giant cane and another of dark green foliage bearing masses of strawberry red flowers. Birds winged in and out—Samoan fantails, pygmy parrots, sunbirds, and other species she'd never seen before. She whistled. She hadn't taken Kaleb's suggestion of trying to train Tasi, so what did she expect? That the beautiful bird would come swooping miraculously out of the trees? The thought was as foolish as her predicament.

Hordes of butterflies met her along the border of a tiny savanna, and she couldn't deny their beauty. They ranged from the very tiny to the magnificent with wingspreads beyond belief, grouping in colors of bright orange, blue, white, and green. They swooshed and soared, landing on purple flowers that poked up between the creeping vanilla and low-lying ferns.

Susan was hungry, but except for a cluster of bananas she found, she had no way of knowing what was edible. Water wasn't a problem. Little springs bubbled up at random with water so clear and cool, it seemed enough to revive the weariest of hearts.

Looking back, she couldn't recall when the landscape began to change. One minute she was struggling along breathing hot, humid air, and the next minute clear sunlight washed across her face. The green canopy was gone, and in its place shone a brilliant blue sky. Her pulse bagan to race. The scenery was familiar yet she couldn't pinpoint it. Afraid that it was an illusion, she began to run. She'd taken only a few hurried, careless steps when she hit a slight dip in the ground and a low-growing tree branch head-on. The last thing she thought before she hit the ground was what slithering creatures might come upon her unconscious body.

At the touch of warmth on her cheek, Susan's violet eyes flew open. Kaleb's handsome face fluttered over her. Was she dead and in heaven, floating in a world of dreams and fantasies?

"You little idiot!" Kaleb growled, his voice a mixture of anger and relief. "If you weren't in such sad shape, I'd whack the daylights out of you!"

Her eyes focused on his face, and what she saw tore at her heart. He knelt above her, his clothing torn and his hair matted. His face was dirty and gashed, and his eyes, a deep green, were filled with pain. "My God," she groaned, trying to sit up.

"Forget it," he muttered through his teeth. "You've sprained an ankle from the looks of the swelling, and you've got a lump on your head the size of a grapefruit. God only knows what else is wrong with you. Stay put while I find a way to get you home."

Susan closed her eyes, the pain returning in sick-ening waves. "I—I saw palm trees and a waterfall. I thought I was almost home so I ran."

"Your downfall, love," he returned, adjusting something under her head. "You weren't watching where you were going." He sighed deeply. "You apparently tripped and fell headlong into a tree."

"What's on the other side of the little hill?" she asked, trying to rid her mind and body of everything but the fact that Kaleb was by her side and she was safe.

"More of the same. Though, if you must know, you were headed in the right direction. You headed overland, that's all."

"You—You look terrible," she whimpered, her heart nearly breaking with the realization that he must have been out searching for her all night.

"And I feel worse, but I'd rather not discuss it. The first priority is to call off the hunt and get you home. Maybe then something can be salvaged of the festivities at the village. Some fia fia with the whole village out looking for you!"

Susan flinched as he spat out each angry word. "I-I'm sorry."

"A little too late for that," he grumbled. "Would you mind telling me why you took off that way? Luina said you were going to the village, but there has to be more to it than that. Nobody could get lost between the reef and the village."

Nobody but her, she thought dismally. But under the circumstances, how could she tell him the truth? It was enough that he was angry with her for wanting to return to the village. What would he say if he knew she'd planned to escape on Moonflight? "I didn't feel well," she lied. "I'm sorry."

"You've already said that. If you didn't feel well, any one of the villagers would've helped you. Even I was within calling range. Damn you and your stubbornness! This—This *thing* you have for independence."

"And what happened to you?" she asked, suddenly angered by his attitude. She'd apologized. Everything that had happened had been her fault, so couldn't he show a little compassion and understanding? What did she have to do to turn him into a human being? "You look as though you've just come through a war. To hear you talk, I'm hardly worth that kind of effort."

"Then that makes two of us who are idiots," he snapped. "Now lay still while I try and wrap your ankle in what's left of my shirt. And I'll have to find you a crutch of sorts. We still have a ways to go and I'll be damned if I'm going to carry you."

"You don't look like you could carry a fly," she flung back at him. Damn him! Her head throbbed, and his caustic words only added to her misery. His hands were raw and bleeding, and despite the throb in her head and the pain in her ankle, and her all-consuming anger, she longed to reach out and kiss away his pain. She longed to tell him how much she loved him. She glared at him instead.

He paid little attention, just wrapped her ankle, tying the makeshift bandage in place with a shoelace and then finding a limb of appropriate length. "Your crutch," he grumbled. "I'll support you on one side, but you'll have to do the rest."

"You mean hop along on one foot and give myself a worse headache? I'd rather stay here!"

He just looked at her, his green eyes the color of the jungle around them. "Do you have a better idea?"

he asked finally, almost gently.

Susan felt a lump form in her throat. "No, I don't have a better idea, but don't go all soft on me. If you give me one shred of sympathy, I'm going to end up blubbering, and that will make my head ache more than hopping along on one foot like a damned rabbit. Let's go, if we must."

As he helped her to her feet, she swayed against him. "I . . . Everything is turning black!" She clutched at his arm while the ground came up to meet her.

She awoke to a cooling breeze across her cheeks, and Laelia's lovely face hovering close by. Was she in bed in the tree house? Her thoughts were tangled, confused. How had she gotten here? She moved her arms and legs and groaned. Every bone and muscle ached.

"Stay still, Miss Susan," Laelia urged. "The doctor said you must stay still."

"The doctor?" Susan's eyes opened wide. She was in bed but not in the tree house. This was a massive bed with dark sides and a footboard. The room was masculine, with guns and trophies on the wall. The aroma of Kaleb's after shave wafted through the air. "Where . . ." She tried to get up, but Laelia held her firm.

"You are in Mr. Kaleb's room," she said softly. "You must be cared for and it would be too difficult if you were in the house in the tree."

"Then Kaleb is staying in the tree house?"

"For now. I will tell Miss Helen you are awake."

"Laelia, please, how did I get here? I was in the jungle with Kaleb."

"Mr. Kaleb carried you. He had a doctor come from Tutuila."

"How long have I been unconscious?" Susan held her breath. She somehow knew it had been a long time.

"Two days, but Doctor Upolu said that is normal for someone with a concussion."

"A concussion?" She groaned and burrowed into the pillow.

"The doctor will be here again tomorrow. He said if you didn't awaken by then, he would have to take you to a hospital." She smiled brightly. "But you are awake. Everyone has been very worried."

Did that include Kaleb? Susan wondered. "The fia fia, Laelia. I hope it went as planned. I hope I didn't mess it up with my crazy stunt."

The girl lowered her eyes. "It went well. I will get Miss Helen."

Something was wrong. Susan could *feel* it.

"Thank God!" Helen exclaimed, hurrying into the bedroom. Essie was at her heels, and the sight of the two women was as welcome as a spring shower. Susan couldn't help but smile.

Tears glistened in Essie's eyes as she kissed Susan's cheek. "You gave us a good fright for sure, honey, but all is well now, eh?"

"We'll nurse you back to health with Laelia's good cooking," Helen interjected with a smile as brilliant as the sun.

"Is Kaleb okay?" Susan asked, holding her breath again. An unreadable message flickered in their eyes. "Is—Is there something you're not telling me?" The women exchanged glances. "Please! Kaleb was in bad shape himself, and if he had to carry me across the island..."

"Kaleb is fine," Helen responded with a sigh. "Oh, he has some cuts and bruises, but nothing serious."

"Then what?" Susan pressed. "Something is wrong. I can see it in your eyes...I could see it in Laelia's eyes." She was feeling panicky and tried to sit up.

"I think we'd better tell the girl," Essie muttered, "or she's going to think the worst and come right up out of that bed. It's not anything for you to concern yourself with, honey. We're just feeling a little down, that's all. Kaleb is flying back to Arizona as soon as the seaplane can get here from Tutuila."

"I don't know what gets into that son of mine," Helen added, "but then that's Kaleb. He's as unpredictable as a South Pacific storm. He wanted to make sure you'd rallied around, of course, and now that you have...Don't take it personally, dear. If you knew him better, you'd understand."

Susan pressed her hand to her mouth. She understood all right. It just hadn't occurred to her that he might want to leave the island on such short notice. But she shouldn't have expected more. "I think I'm the reason he's leaving," she said, closing her eyes. She wanted to hide the pain she felt, the shattering of her heart. "We haven't been getting along well."

"That nephew of mine should have his rear end tanned," Essie grumbled.

"No...no, it isn't his fault, at least not entirely. We just happen to bring out the worst in each other, that's all. I do understand." She took a deep, haunted breath. "Will I be able to travel by the end of the week?" she asked Essie. Now that it was over, the thought of staying on the island was like a final stake driven into her heart.

"The doctor would like to keep an eye on you for a week or two, honey. But don't worry. There isn't a darned thing in San Francisco that won't keep until you're able to travel. The city will survive without us."

But the question was: Could she survive on the island without Kaleb? Could she survive life anywhere without him?

CHAPTER
Thirteen

DRESSED IN A yellow halter and matching shorts, and with her sketch pad under her arm, Susan hobbled down to the beach. It had been a week since Kaleb had left the island, and her artwork seemed to be the only thing that had kept her from going mad. She was walking without the aid of a crutch now, and even gaining weight, thanks to Laelia's good cooking and Helen and Essie hovering over her like a couple of mother hens. The dark circles under her eyes had begun to fade, but anyone looking closely at her could still see her violet eyes grown dusty with heart-felt sorrow. She knew it would take much more than a week or two to forget Kaleb Knight, if she ever could.

She couldn't bring herself to walk to the section

of beach where the sand was pink and shells spilled
in confusion, where Kaleb had kissed her that first
day. Nor had she been able to return to the tree house.
Even the stable was almost unbearable, but Sam had
helped, allowing her to groom Moonflight. He had
even agreed to another lesson in oils while they'd sat
in the shade of a Jacaranda. No one mentioned Kaleb.
It was as though he had never existed.

Now, sitting on the sand, Susan decided to sketch
the pier. Next week they would be taking off for San
Francisco, and she would leave all of her sketches
and paintings behind.

When she heard the hum of the seaplane, she
looked up, shading her eyes from the sun. It must be
the weekly drop of supplies. Just this morning Helen
had complained about running short of everything.

She watched the seaplane land, glider-soft, and
then taxi up to the pier. She watched the man who
got off just ahead of the pilot, the man whose shimmering copper hair shown like a beacon in the morning
sun. Kaleb! Dear God, it was Kaleb! Her pulse flamed
and her breath quickened. The sky had suddenly
turned bluer than blue, and the water sparkled like
diamonds. Every nerve tingled with awareness.

Kaleb saw her and, without hesitation, strode over
to where she sat. He wore slim tan pants and a pale
yellow shirt. Her gaze rested on his turquoise belt
buckle, and she was very aware he had lost weight.

"Hello, Susan," he greeted her huskily. "You're
looking well."

"Your mother and aunt have taken good care of
me. I think they were looking for an excuse to fatten
me up. Are they expecting you?" Her voice sounded
far away.

"No, it'll be a surprise. How are your injuries?"

"Better. I can walk without a crutch now, and I haven't had a headache in days."

His jade eyes flickered over the tumble of chestnut hair atop her head and moved down to her trim ankles. Her eyes moved from his belt buckle to his face and then to his hands. Traces of his wounds were still visible. He sat down beside her, digging the heels of his boots into the sand.

"Why did you come back?" she asked in the same far away voice.

"I went off without my manuscript."

"Your mother could have mailed it to you."

"And I didn't say good-bye."

The sudden sheen in his eyes caught her off guard. Their eyes met and locked. The sun touched his russet hair.

She took a deep breath, trembling. "Good-byes can be a dreadful bore. It's just as well you didn't. Makes it easier for me to hate you."

His voice lowered. "And do you hate me?"

"What would you do if I said yes?"

"I wouldn't believe you." He took her hands and pulled her to her feet. "Come on, let's take a walk."

They moved down the beach slowly, allowing for Susan's ankle. His arms were supportive, tender, but when she realized they were heading for that special stretch of beach, she stopped. "I-I can't."

"Can't what? Is it your ankle?" When she didn't reply, he swept her up in his arms and carried her the remaining distance, then set her down gently.

"I don't want to be here," she murmured on a strangle of air.

His face hovered dangerously close. "Why not, my

teinetiti? I thought this was one of your favorite spots on the island."

"It is. It was. But it brings back too many painful memories. We were friends the last time we were here."

"And then somewhere it went wrong. Our friendship...our relationship. It was hell for me too, though I don't expect you to believe that."

She shook her head almost frantically. "I don't know what to believe. I only know that every time I'm near you I find myself losing control, and then I end up hating myself as well."

"Why? Because with every breath you want me as desperately as I want you? Why did you run away that night on the reef?" His eyes moved over her face, slowly, sensually. "Was it because you were afraid that when the fishing was over, I'd sweep you up in my arms and carry you off to some dark, secluded spot and make passionate love to you?"

"That was part of it." Her legs felt shaky under her.

"And the rest?"

She stood on the pink sand on the beach she loved beside the man she loved, and knew it was time for truth. "I couldn't accept a relationship based on nothing more than physical attraction," she said painfully. "I would never be able to accept a casual affair. I was wrong to let you make love to me that night in the stable. It was a moment of madness. Sex without love is nothing more than a biological urge, and all too easily forgotten."

"An urge too strong to deny," Kaleb said, slowly pulling her into his arms. "Do you see how easily you fall into my arms? Can't you feel the magic force of two bodies wanting to become one?"

"What I see is a foolish woman who has fallen in love with an impossible man," Susan sighed wearily. "A man who has a heart of stone. To continue a relationship on those terms could only mean my downfall. Though my heart ached when you left last week, I knew it was for the best. Oh, God, Kaleb, why did you come back?"

"Because I love you, too, my little fool," he groaned, smothering her face with kisses. "What hell you've put me through. Why do you think I came back? I'm as guilty as you are, it seems. I ran away because I couldn't face the truth. But when I stepped off the plane in Arizona, I knew it wouldn't work. Running away is for the fools of the world, and although I may be many things, I've never considered myself a fool."

Dazed, Susan could only stare up at him. "You also told me love is for fools," she reminded him.

"Ah, but that was the first day, my beautiful violet-eyed minx. Before I discovered what it means to truly love. I can't tell you when it happened. One minute you were Susan McRay, an adorable, adventuresome young woman I wanted to protect, and the next, you were the woman I desired with all my heart. I thought that would be enough for a while, but my feelings were growing by such proportions, I could no longer deny them. One morning I woke up and there it was. I knew I loved you, and it scared the hell out of me. I didn't know how to handle it. The night I went charging around the jungle like a madman searching for you, I realized I couldn't go on. It was time to get the hell out while I still had my skin."

"Oh, Kaleb," Susan whispered, collapsing against

him. "If—If I'd had even the smallest hint of how you really felt."

"You should have by the way I reacted to your friendship with Sam. I'd never known jealousy before. It was new to me and baffling."

They blended together then, a molding of their bodies as one. When his mouth hungrily overtook hers, she felt as though she had come home. It was the bliss she had dreamed of, the world had just begun. This was day one, a new life.

"You'll have to marry me so everyone will get off my back," Kaleb murmured against her hair. "You have no idea what I've been up against. It seems everyone on the island had us in love and married before I realized what was happening. Even my mother and Aunt Essie. They were none too happy when I took off, but they said I'd be back. Will you marry me, my teinetiti? Will you become my island bride and make my life complete with the beauty and fulfillment every man dreams about but rarely finds?"

Susan nodded, knowing another stone had been turned. With a tremulous smile she whispered, "I'll marry you, Kaleb. I don't think I could survive without your love."

He silenced her with a kiss that held the promise of every tomorrow.

Second Chance at Love™

**Please turn
the page
for our questionnaire
and an exciting**

SECOND CHANCE
AT LOVE

offer!!!

QUESTIONNAIRE

1. How many romances do you buy each month
   - ☐ 5 or less
   - ☐ 5 to 10
   - ☐ more than 10

2. Do you like, primarily
   - ☐ modern-day romances
   - ☐ Regency period romances
   - ☐ both, equally
   - ☐ other historical romances

3. Were the love scenes in this novel
   - ☐ too explicit
   - ☐ not explicit enough
   - ☐ handled tastefully

4. Do you prefer stories set
   - ☐ in the USA
   - ☐ in foreign countries
   - ☐ both, equally

5. How old do you like your heroines to be
   - ☐ 17 to 22
   - ☐ 23 to 27
   - ☐ 28 to 32
   - ☐ 33 to 40
   - ☐ over 40

6. The length of this book is
   - ☐ too short
   - ☐ just right
   - ☐ too long

7. The main reason I buy a romance is
   - ☐ a friend's recommendation
   - ☐ a bookseller's recommendation
   - ☐ because of the cover
   - ☐ other reason:_____

8. Where did you buy this book?
   - ☐ chain store (drug, department, etc.)
   - ☐ bookstore
   - ☐ supermarket
   - ☐ other:_____

9. Mind telling your age?
   Our lips are sealed…
   - ☐ under 18
   - ☐ 18 to 30
   - ☐ 31 to 45
   - ☐ over 45

10. Check here if you would like to
    - ☐ receive the SECOND CHANCE AT LOVE Newsletter

. . . .

Fill-in your name and address below:

name:_____

street address:_____

city_____ state_____ zip_____

Please share your other ideas about romances with us on an additional sheet and attach it securely to this questionnaire.

PLEASE RETURN THIS QUESTIONNAIRE TO:
SECOND CHANCE AT LOVE, THE BERKLEY/JOVE PUBLISHING GROUP
200 Madison Avenue, New York, New York 10016

Second Chance at Love ™

All of the above titles are $1.75 per copy